Nightmares

Edited by R. Edgewood

Published by 53rd Street Publishing

Offices in Gibsons, B.C. Canada and Lincoln City, Oregon

Nightmares

Edited by R. Edgewood

Published by 53rd Street Publishing

Cover art © Shannon Beauford | Dreamstime.com

Cover designed by R. Edgewood

Cover design and layout 2015 by 53rd Street Publishing
ISBN 978-1-927621-45-5

53rd Street Publishing

Head office: Gibsons B.C. Canada

www.53rdstreetpublishing.com

This is a work of fiction. Any similarities to persons living or dead are purely coincidental.

In the future, lack of belief is the undead's greatest weapon.....

Today the hunt is a loner's profession, so I don't think about the old days much anymore. When I crave rich, fresh blood, my memories fade like a morning mist. Not that I've seen a morning in a long time. In fact, it's a memory that is badly faded.

Back in the day, humans still believed in the supernatural and good and evil. These days, the humans worship science instead of God. They don't believe in the undead. They think vampires are a myth from bedtime stories and all I am is a simple serial killer. Perpetuating this myth is my greatest disguise.

I knelt next to my kill, tilted its head back to expose the pale throat, and then sank my fangs into its yielding flesh. The warm, life-giving blood immediately flowed down my throat. I drank until I sensed the old one's heart had stopped.

I stood and ran my index finger around my mouth to wipe the excess blood off my lips, then sucked the remnants off my finger as if it were an elixir. I closed my eyes and purred my satisfaction, savoring the moment.

Old blood is the best. I estimated the prey's age to be at least forty, maybe even a little older. A good vintage.

Acknowledgments

Thank you to our editor, Colleen Kuehne, for her diligent efforts to improve our work. We are forever grateful to her and to the late, late shows everywhere that keep the old horror movies alive for the inspiration.

Dedication

For Forrest J. Ackerman and the editors and contributors to *Eerie* and *Creepy Magazines* that sparked so many imaginations.

Table of Contents

Introduction

When you are editing an anthology of horror, you want to cover a range of styles and types of horror. We have tried to encompass a range of popular archetypes while staying true to our initial vision of favorite monsters across all media. Hence we have man-made monsters, mad scientists, vampires, werewolves, and ghosts. Hopefully you will enjoy these tales and even experience a few nightmares because of them.

Thank you for taking time to read this volume. Look for other collections from 53rd Street Publishing. We publish fiction for everyone.

R. Edgewood
August 2015

This is the second short story about Aloha Armstrong, The Woman from L.I.P.S., a secret agent who fights for freedom in the strangest of circumstances. Aloha first appeared in the novel My Zombie Prince, *available as an ebook, in print online, or at your favorite bookstore. This story takes place after the events of the novel in an alternate reality where monsters are normal.*

Big Hairy Deal

R.G. Hart

FOR ONCE I WASN'T IN THE OFFICE when our future four-legged client bounded past me, snarling at screaming civilians. At the time I was concentrating on squeezing a grapefruit at Mo's Fruitland on Bleeker Street, near the office.

My office is located on the third floor of a three-story, mold-covered brick walk-up above Bleeker Street in the city of Vancouver. And not the pretty, multi-cultural-Mecca Vancouver by the sea you're thinking of—the one on the west coast of Canada. My Vancouver is the one sucked into the dark, gloomy, alternate reality where paranormal is normal.

Today was a day like most days. I was squeezing fruit, watching a crazed vendor swinging a broom in self-defense at a werewolf, and I knew I had to do something about it. It's my job.

1

Big Hairy Deal

With my partner, I own and operate a private detective agency. We solve problems in the neighborhood. Unusual problems. No, not plumbing or electrical problems, those are someone else's problem. We deal with the who-ya-gonna-call kinda problems.

In an alternate universe, I used to be an agent for the Legal Investigative Protection Service. Yes, I am the original Woman From L.I.P.S. Impressive, I know, but when Matt and I were accidentally sucked into a space-time portal, we ended up here where the L.I.P.S. doesn't exist. A girl with my skills has to have something to do, so naturally we became PIs.

Matt Butcher, former zombie and my some-time boyfriend, is my partner in our little two-person agency, Abby-Normal Investigations.

Our motto is: We take on any case no matter how weird, how supernatural, how small, how big, or how much you want to pay. Justice is our middle name.

My middle name is actually Mabel, but I hate it.

I introduce myself using only my first and last names. "Armstrong, Aloha Armstrong, Private Dick" has a nice ring to it. Aloha Mabel Armstrong? Yuck.

As far as I'm concerned, my middle name is as big a secret as the combination on the suitcase with the nuclear launch codes.

Anyway, Matt and I handle the cases the cops are too scared to, or the ones they have no idea how to. Our clients are mostly zombies, vampires, midgets (some of my best friends are midgets), swamp monsters, and all sorts of alien life-forms. Let me tell you, aliens are the worst tippers. Anyone got change for a Zelbot drudge?

Yeah, sure, every once in a while a real person walks through the door, but they're usually looking for the can.

So today, as I was squeezing the grapefruit, this werewolf suddenly appeared and started tearing up the fruit stand and threatening to eat the customers. Since I'm a lot like Batman (other than the shoulder-length, copper-red, wavy hair; knee-high, spike-heeled leather boots; leather mini-skirt; and midriff-baring, too-tight tee, we are exactly the same), I carry every sort of utility item in my purse. Naturally, I came to the rescue.

I pulled a werewolf biscuit from my purse and quickly had this werewolf understanding who's the alpha. In fact, soon the beast was on its back, whimpering like a puppy, and I was scratching its belly.

It didn't take long before there was the inevitable shape shift and a naked woman lay at my feet and I was scratching her belly. OK, I know this sounds weird (and it is), but in this universe weird is my business.

I stood. "You OK?"

She blinked, with her arms and legs still in air in that aren't-I-the-cute-little-puppy position, then said, "Yeah, I think so." A frown creased her brow. "But I'm not sure."

I sensed there was more to this woman's story, I just needed to dig a little deeper. I needed Matt.

***

Once back at the office, I made a cup of green tea for our prospective client while Matt gave her a blanket to cover herself. She was shivering by now, not a surprise given it rains most of the year here. I glanced out the window overlooking Bleeker Street in time to see a flash of lightning brighten the gray, overcast sky. Really? Does it have to be gloomy all the time?

Our office is located downtown in the seedier section of the city, in a building way past its prime. Not that it's going to be here much longer.

Foreign developers bought blocks of downtown a few years back and have built several towers of condos in the midst of the cesspool. For eight hundred grand, you get a closet with a great view of another closet with a great view. Did I buy one of these expensive shoeboxes? Yeah, right. I may work with the undead but I'm not brain dead.

Anyway, the woman, Lizzie Harris, turned out to be an accountant for a mad scientist bent on world domination.

Why anyone would want to dominate this world is beyond me. The place is such a mess, you'd have to spend all your time running around fixing stuff. Like I'm the handy-woman type? I don't think so.

Matt, with his calm demeanor, was, as usual, able to elicit information Lizzie didn't realize she even knew. Square-jawed Matt, with his wavy brown hair, intense hazel eyes, and aura of confident strength makes most women weak at the knees. He's beautiful and he's mine. At least for now.

In the dark days before Zombie Away, Matt suffered from zombieitis. I often wonder if his inner calm comes from his days as a zombie. He seemed so carefree when we first met. Maybe, if you know you're going to turn to dust soon, you have a different outlook on life. I'm no shrink, so what do I know?

Our on-again, off-again relationship suffers because he has no sense of humor. He's so darned serious all the time and it drives me nuts. He says I'm too sarcastic to be a good detective. It's our sore point.

Lizzie told us the mad scientist has been cooking the books and stealing from his investors. Who knew mad scientists had investors?

I sat, half listening to her explanation of his embezzlement scheme, thinking about my hair appointment this afternoon, not particularly caring about any of this (you invest in the evil scheme of a crazed genius, what do you expect?) until she said he also applied for some government research grants under false pretenses.

"I think you just threw us a bone," I blurted, silencing Matt and Lizzie.

Lizzie looked at me slack-jawed and the corners of Matt's mouth curled slightly, then dropped back into the familiar grim line. He'd never admit it but I just made him laugh.

"Is that a crack?" Lizzie asked indignantly.

Oops. Time for damage control. "Huh? Sorry. No, not at all." I tried my best let's-be-pals smile but she glared at me. Her angular features were pinched like she'd sucked on a lemon. Werewolves can be touchy about their inner wild child.

"What I'm referring to is the part about your boss ripping off the government. I don't like that." I lowered my voice. "I mean I really don't like that."

Lizzie shriveled deeper into the worn wing chair and gripped her teacup tighter, causing the color to drain from her knuckles. I swear I saw fear in her eyes. A frightened werewolf is just pitiful.

I may have gone too intense, but then sometimes you have to let the client know you're not all sweetness and light. It's especially important, when you're a hot-looking babe like me, that people see your serious side.

Matt gazed at me and gave me the slight nod he does when he's telling me to cool it. He rolled his shoulders beneath his perfectly tailored double-breasted suit, then shifted his gaze to Lizzie.

"Sorry about her. She gets a little carried away." He paused to clear his throat. "What she means is that the government will pay us to find out more about your boss's embezzlement scheme."

Lizzie grinned at him like a schoolgirl on her first date. I suppressed the urge to gag, and crossed my arms over my bosom, determined to keep quiet.

Matt continued. "What's your boss's name?"

"He's quite mad, you know?"

Matt nodded.

"His name's Tres Zero."

***

The Zeros have been haunting us since we started this agency. In fact, even before that when we stopped the father, Arnold Zero, from stealing the formula for Zombie Away. Then we stopped his son Uno when he threatened to turn the whole world into zombies.

A Google search confirmed Tres Zero is the illegitimate son of Uno Zero and the bearded lady from the Ding-a-ling Brothers' Circus.

Yup, we're up to our necks in Zeros again.

This simple case of embezzlement had suddenly turned into a race against time to stop another Zero from taking over the world.

My heart pounded in my ears and my blood coursed through my veins. It's days like this when ya know this crime-fighting gig just never gets old.

***

We arrived at Castle Zero, situated at the end of a winding, dirt road atop Mount Seymour overlooking the city, just as dusk fell.

When you live in a place where weather is an issue, let me tell you that dusk falls hard. The night was as black as the inside of a cookie jar. Not that I know what the inside of a cookie jar looks like, but a girl can dream, even when she's always on a diet.

Matt was driving. The '74 Pinto rattled and wheezed its way along the winding road up the side of the mountain. Pelting rain bounced off the roof of the rusting hulk of a car. We finally came to a stop outside the ten-foot high front gates guarding a long gravel driveway that I hoped led to the castle beyond. It was so dark now, seeing much of anything beyond the gate was a best guess.

The Pinto sighed as if it were relieved to get this far.

No kidding, me too.

It often occurs to me our car might be haunted, which wouldn't be surprising, but that investigation would have to wait for another day. We had tax fraud and a take-over-the-world case going right now so our plate was full, thank you very much. No room for the small stuff.

Besides, Lizzie said she'd pay mucho dollars to get the goods on her boss. And when we have the evidence of fraud, we'll turn it over to the government. They pay handsome rewards for stuff like that.

I'm hoping it's enough so Matt and I can take the big vacation we always talk about—or rather, I talk about. He just listens, occasionally grunts, and nods.

And then there's the whole saving the world thing. That's gonna be icing on the cake. I mean, we're talking about a mad scientist, not a rocket scientist, how serious could it be?

Big Hairy Deal

The Pinto's four cylinders chugged and the fan belt whined and squeaked as I stared through the streaky windshield at the gates. Along the tops of the steel bars were images of hissing gargoyles and a grinning fairy with a mouth full of razor-sharp teeth. Not the most inviting thing I'd ever seen, but not the worst either.

These weren't like those hideous smiling clowns of Slashing, Montana. I shivered. That's an image I'd rather forget, but never can.

"There's an intercom," Matt said, with a nod of his head at the stone wall next to the gates. I squinted into the darkness. Sure enough, through the shimmering rain I saw a square black pad with an oval-shaped, lemon-yellow button affixed to the wall about knee high from the ground.

"Oh, you've got to be kidding." This Zero is a chip off the old woodpile. The button being where it is means he's a little person, too. It seems in the Zero family all the fruit hangs close to the ground. "Not too far to fall, I guess," I muttered.

"What?" said Matt.

"Nothing. It's a joke."

He nodded, his face hard as steel. "You gonna get us in?"

I had flipped a coin on the drive here to determine who would get out if there were a gate. I lost. I looked down at my expensive leather boots, then at the muddy road, then at Matt. I think he knew there'd be a gate.

I swung the car door open, then pulled my plastic raincoat over my head and ran to the wall. Mud squished underfoot and the smells of the surrounding fir and pine trees and the musty rain filled my senses.

Before I pressed the intercom button, I noticed what looked like a coin slot on the panel, something I hadn't noticed from the car. Odd.

Never seen a coin slot on an intercom before. I shrugged and pressed the button.

I waited while rainwater dripped off my coat all around me, and shuffled my feet so my precious leather boots wouldn't sink any deeper into the sucking mud. After what seemed like forever, a gravel-crunching voice came over the intercom.

"Yeah?"

I'd practiced various pitches all the way here. I knew Matt grew tired of listening when he started saying every one was pitch perfect, even though some were just stupid and off key.

"Hi, we're from Publishers Habitat Sweepstakes. We have a check for Dear Occupant." I took my finger off the button.

Girl, when your wit is on, it's really on.

There was a slight pause, then the voice said, "Mr. Occupant doesn't wish to be disturbed. Go away."

I pressed the button again and laughed. "No, wait. Please. That was just a little sweepstakes humor we use around the office. Actually, I have a big fat check for a Mr. Tres Zero. Would Mr. Zero be at home?" Again, I released the button.

I could feel it in my bones, this was gonna work for sure.

There was another pause, only longer this time, then the voice said, "Put fifty cents in the slot and come up to the house. Greta will meet you." The tinny speaker crackled, then fell silent.

Yeah, baby you are *sooo* smooth.

It was then I realized I didn't have any coins on me, and for sure not in my I'm-so-cool-I'm-tiny purse back in the car. I glanced at the slot. It didn't look like it took bills. I looked to the car with its fading headlights and sagging suspension.

I hoped Matt had exact change.

Big Hairy Deal
***

We came back in two hours. Thankfully, the gas station we had passed at the bottom of the mountain was still open. The snag-toothed attendant even pumped gas for us so we could get the change we needed. Ever try to pump exactly two dollars and fifty cents' worth of gas? It ain't easy.

After we got back, I first buzzed the house to let them know we had returned, then slipped the coins into the slot.

I ran to the passenger's side of the Pinto and climbed in, wincing as the tall gates slowly opened on ear-splitting hinges.

Once past the gates, the Pinto groaned and popped as it crunched over the gravel driveway. I winced as a rock pinged off the undercarriage. The car had to last another year, at least until I've made the final payment.

Finally, we stopped on the circular driveway in front of the two-story ink-black mansion. There were stone steps leading to a heavy oak door with a gargoyle knocker. A row of twenty-foot marble columns stood on either side of the steps holding an overhang off the sloped roof. The mansion reminded me of Scarlet O'Hara's in *Gone With the Wind* crossed with the *Addams Family* house.

We got out and walked up the steps to the door. I was grateful for the overhang; it kept us out of the rain.

Matt tipped the edge of his fedora to let the excess rain fall off—I really love when he wears his hat; it makes him look all Sam Spade—then used the gargoyle knocker to announce us. As the echo of the thump, thump dissipated, the door began to swing aside. They must have oiled the hinges recently because it did so soundlessly.

I expected the interior to be as gloomy as the exterior but was surprised to find a well-kept foyer with a polished wood floor, a maroon and navy Persian rug, and a rosewood side table with a matching chair beside it. On the table was an antique lamp that cast a soft glow over the woman who greeted us.

A gentle smile played across her thin lips. "Hello, Mr. Butcher and Miss Armstrong," she said, gazing at us over her reading glasses in a way reminiscent of a schoolmarm. She was short—no more than four feet eleven—with grey hair pulled into a tight bun atop her oval-shaped head. Her navy and red paisley dress ran past her knees and hung loosely on her small frame, and on her tiny feet she wore plain black slip-on shoes.

"I'm the doctor's housemaid, Greta."

"Hello, Greta," I said, deciding in the interests of time to use the direct approach I'm best known for. "We're here to see the doc. We hear he's planning on taking over the world."

A puzzled frown formed on Greta's forehead. "I'm sorry, dear, but I don't know what you're talking about. Dr. Zero is trying to help people."

Matt interrupted before I could rebut the old lady. "Sorry, Greta, my partner gets a little carried away sometimes." He glanced at me and raised an eyebrow.

Oh, I get it. Good detective, bad detective. I nodded, but scowled at him to add to the illusion I was angry. Which I actually was, but since it enhanced my role as the bad dick, I decided to play along.

Greta smiled at Matt in that creepy, cougar-like way. I swear Matt could charm the pants off Ann Coulter on her worst day.

He continued. "We've come a long way to see Mr. Zero." He patted the left breast of his suit jacket. "We have the check."

Big Hairy Deal

"Yes, of course. I'll take you to his laboratory." She turned and started to walk away. "Right this way."

She led us through the quiet house filled with more antique furniture and Persian rugs, the woods floors polished and gleaming. We passed a grandfather clock that chimed the half hour. The black arms on the brass face told me it was eleven thirty already.

Finally, she led us into a massive library with floor-to-ceiling shelves filled with hardcover books. I stared at the old lady. Is she kidding? The secret entrance to a mad scientist's laboratory in the library is so old school it's a cliché.

She walked to another door at the other end of the room, then used a brass key she withdrew from the pocket of her dress to unlock it. She swung it open and inside was the laboratory, complete with a workbench with racks of test tubes and humming machines for I-don't-know-what, and a man who could only be Dr. Tres Zero.

His lab is on the first floor, not the dusty basement? Sometimes even *I* can be wrong.

As I suspected, Tres Zero was a little person with slicked, oil-black hair, a neatly trimmed goatee, and a mustache. He wore a gray vest under his white lab coat and white running shoes on his feet. To me he looked more like a miniature version of Sigmund Freud than a mad scientist, but looks can be deceiving.

"Hello," said Zero with a grin, his thumbs hooked in the pockets of his vest. A chain from a pocket watch hung across his belly between the vest pockets. "Can I have the check, please? I have a lot of work to do before midnight."

Midnight! That must be zero hour. (Come on, you know someone had to say it.)

"What happens at midnight?" asked Matt, his hazel eyes casually scanning the laboratory.

12

"You two and the others will be my slaves," Zero said, like he was ordering a skinny latté with a twist.

My stomach muscles tightened. We were about to take a trip on the crazy train. Good thing Matt's the Boy Scout of our little agency. He always comes prepared.

Glancing at the old woman, I saw her begin to shape shift. The old lady gave way to a snarling, flesh-eating werewolf, and I was fresh out of werewolf biscuits.

Matt reached into his suit jacket and pulled out his .45 automatic. Without warning, he turned the gun on the old-lady-werewolf and shot her twice. Once in the chest, again in the middle of her forehead. The first shot stopped her in her tracks, the other blew out the back of her head, scattering her brains across the lab. The bullets slammed her backward and she landed hard, then shifted back to her human form. It wasn't a pretty sight.

"Silver bullets?" I asked.

Matt shrugged. "Of course."

In the commotion, Zero ducked under the laboratory bench and disappeared into a trap door in the floor.

Suddenly gas jets lit up with blue and red flames along the perimeter of the walls. Like all mad scientists, Zero had a self-destruct-when-discovered obsession so the house and all its contents, including the evidence of fraud, was going up in flames. If we wanted to avoid going up with it, we needed to leave right now. There'd be no time to search the house.

We may have stopped Zero's evil plan for world domination, whatever it was, but our payday was gone.

***

Big Hairy Deal

The next day we sat in the office with our feet on top of our desks discussing the Zero case, hoping the next client would soon darken our door.

"What do you think Zero was up to?"

Matt shrugged, then took a sip from his Mickey Mouse coffee mug. "Werewolves, I'd say."

"Werewolves?"

"Yeah, ya know, a big hairy deal."

I looked at him and his features were as serious as ever. "You know you just made a joke, right?"

He shook his head. "Nope."

I sighed. "Someday you're gonna slip, and I'm gonna be there to laugh my butt off."

This is the debut story of paranormal investigator Amanda Dark and her adventures helping tormented ghosts cross over to their final destinations. Look for other Amanda Dark stories in this volume.

Hook Island
An Amanda Dark Paranormal Mystery

R.G. Hart

AMANDA HELD OUT THE FLASHLIGHT, but the muddy beam of light barely penetrated the inky, thick darkness more than a few feet ahead. Her heart beat loudly in her ears as she carefully stepped forward on the rickety, wooden dock. She glanced over her left shoulder to see Pierre in the launch he'd used to bring her to this isolated island off the coast of South Carolina. She swallowed hard and for the hundredth time doubted she'd made the right decision.

"Pierre!" she called. "Which way?"

Squinting into the nearly impenetrable darkness, Amanda could just barely make out Pierre's shape, bathed in the glow from the instruments in the dash of the boat. Pierre had been at first understandably reluctant, but once she flashed a hundred-dollar bill, he had readily agreed to transport her to Hook Island. The transplanted Cajun, originally from New Orleans until Hurricane Katrina, was amiable and friendly during the ride from Isle of Palms. She sensed he thought she had a screw loose, but if anyone had told her she would make such a trip in the dead of night, she might have agreed with them.

Hook Island

"Straight ahead!" She heard his voice echo over the sound of the rhythmic waves ahead of her in the darkness.

Amanda swiveled her head back and forth, still unable to see her way along the dock. Her night vision was terrible—a definite problem for a paranormal investigator who often worked at night. Her breathing was rapid and her mouth and nose were filled with the smell of wet sand, salt air, and the acidic odor of rotting seaweed. "Too bad I can't lose my sense of smell on command," she mused under her breath.

She carefully moved one foot ahead; the boards creaked. If she didn't walk off the edge of the old dock, no doubt it would collapse beneath her.

She should have come in the daytime, but the letter had said it was a matter of life and death. She had seen enough ghosts to know death intimately, so she had dropped everything back home in Boston and caught the first plane to Charleston. Of course, the certified check for five thousand dollars certainly added to her motivation to come quickly.

Such a large deposit surprised her until she did some research on the plane using her iPad. According to the websites she surfed, her mysterious benefactor, Phillip Swann, was a descendant of the notorious pirate, Captain Henry "Blackblood" Swann, who sailed these waters in the mid-eighteenth century. Captain Swann pillaged French, British, and Spanish ships for gold, silver, slaves, coffee, and anything else of value. There were suggestions that once he captured a vessel, he set the crew adrift in lifeboats before setting fire to their ships. This last part of the legend was unconfirmed, but if true, then Swann wasn't as despicable as many of his contemporaries.

R.G. Hart

Her problem right now wasn't proving the truth behind the musty legend, it was surviving the trip from the dock to the Swann family house, somewhere on this speck of sand and rock. She'd survived worse, but not being able to see where she was going in pitch blackness had always been her greatest fear.

The light from her flashlight flickered twice, then went out. *Just great*, she thought. *Now what am I gonna do?*

She stuck the tip of her tongue out one side of her mouth and concentrated on her footing. She then took one step and heard a crack as her foot dropped through a hole in the boards. Oh, oh. Not good.

Trying to extract her foot, she lost her balance and stumbled forward. She lost her grip on the small suitcase in her right hand, and it flew away from her to be lost somewhere in the darkness. A twinge of relief came over her when she heard it land on sand. At least her extra blue jeans, shorts, and tops would be dry. And her iPad and cell phone would still function. Saltwater destroyed electronic gear thoroughly and quickly. Without her equipment, her trip to Hook Island would have been pointless. If there were a ghost, she would need photographic evidence. No photos, no future book; no future book, no food on table. Girl's gotta eat.

Knowing she was about to fall off the dock, she held out her hands, closed her eyes, and got ready to break the inevitable as best she could. Hopefully she wouldn't break anything important. She fell forward and found herself sprawled facedown on sand. Her mouth had filled with the stuff and she spat out the sticky grains as best she could, but the annoying grit was stubborn and wasn't going without a fight. She'd never liked the beach. There was too much sand, too much wind, and too much saltwater for her liking.

When she tried to lift her head, overwhelming dizziness gripped her, accompanied by a wave of nausea. She set her head back on the sand. The feeling passed, but she realized there was a half-buried stone in the sand sticking up. She must have struck her forehead against it. A growing warmth pooled around her forehead, confirming her theory that she was bleeding. The unmistakable odor of blood flooded her nostrils. *Oh, crap. So not good.*

She suppressed the urge to cry. *I'm going to die on a desert island, in the dark, alone.* She investigated the paranormal. She didn't want to be part of it, at least not yet. *I'm too young to die.*

The panic gripping her faded, replaced by rationality. *I need to stop wallowing in self-pity*, she scolded herself. *Just because Paul left with the cat doesn't mean I have to fall to pieces during every tiny crisis. Oh, oh...*

As if a window closed, Amanda's world abruptly disappeared.

***

Amanda's eyes fluttered open, and through fuzzy vision came streaks of filtered sunlight across a wooden ceiling. Her vision cleared and she shifted her head to her left. There was a window, framed by shredded curtains. The glass in the window was missing, so a breeze made the curtains billow like torn rags in the wind.

Shifting her legs, she realized she lay on her back, her head resting on a severely squashed pillow. The air reeked of dust and mildew. Her mouth was devoid of moisture. She ran her tongue over her dry lips, then gradually rose up on her elbows until she sat up. She blinked and her dry eyeballs clicked.

Her head throbbed. Instinctively she placed one hand on the side of her head, and her fingers brushed a bandage wrapped around her wounded noggin. Now she recalled the fall off the dock. It must have been a while ago since it wasn't night anymore—as evidenced by the sunlight creating a spotlight effect on the dirty wood floor.

She froze when, from a corner of her left eye, she saw movement. Looking down, she saw a black cat with a white-tipped tail padding across the room. Unable to look away, Amanda watched the cat until it vanished into the wall.

Her heart beat a little harder and she sucked in a breath. The cat hadn't been real, at least not anymore. It was a ghost.

Amanda had seen strange things, but never an actual ghost. Most of the paranormal activity she'd witnessed was minor stuff: objects moving by themselves, sudden fluctuations in room temperature, mysterious breezes on a calm night, and things that go bump in the night. She'd never seen a real, live ghost. Uh...correction, a real dead ghost.

Amanda let her head sink back to the pillow and closed her eyes. *I must be seeing things...*

"Hello, Miss Dark?"

Amanda's eyes popped open. Standing at the side of the bed was a square-jawed man, his chin and cheeks covered in dark stubble. His jet black, curly hair was cut short and his eyes were as blue as a Caribbean sea. His lips formed a wry smile and his eyes twinkled.

"Uh...yeah...I'm Amanda Dark." Her brow wrinkled as she eyed the man. "Are you Phillip Swann?"

He nodded. "You really didn't have to come out here in the middle of the night."

She cringed inside. He was correct, of course, but for some reason she had sensed that he needed her as soon as possible.

She had no idea where the sense of urgency had come from, just that it had. "You're right, of course, Mr. Swann."

He chuckled. "Mr. Swann was my father. Please call me Phillip."

His smile disappeared and he arched one eyebrow, sending a shiver of longing through her. She hadn't had a steady boyfriend since high school, when, immediately after the grad party, Dave Allister had announced he was going back east to college and had broken up with her. He had broken her heart. That was, of course, after they'd had sex.

Since then she'd dated occasionally, but nothing stuck. Of course, after college she'd become a paranormal investigator. Men didn't seem to like women who chased dead things. When Paul (her only serious boyfriend after Dave) left, he had made that much clear.

"Hello, Phillip." She held out her right hand, which he grasped lightly in his as they shook hands. His warm, gentle touch sent shock waves of desire through her, unlike anything she'd ever experienced; not even with Dave in the back seat of his father's Durango back in her high school days.

"I thought I'd better come as quickly as possible," she explained. "Your letter said it was a matter of life and death."

Phillip's cheeks glowed crimson, his eyes averted; instead of looking at her, he looked in the direction of the window. He moved toward it and gazed out at the rolling surf of the ocean beyond the few trees that stuck up from the tan-colored sand in front of them.

Amanda rose to a seated position and then swung her legs over the side of the bed. Her head throbbed but she ignored the pain. She came up behind him and detected a sense of sadness emanating from Phillip. For most of her life, she'd had the gift of empathy. She couldn't read thoughts but had a strong sense of feelings.

R.G. Hart

It certainly made her life interesting at times, and not always for the good. Back in high school, she'd managed to avoid the bullies when she detected their feelings toward her. Of course, it didn't hurt when your best friend, Mary Olson, was captain of the lacrosse team. Mary was as tough as any boy and had been known to flatten a few.

Amanda placed a hand on Phillip's shoulder. He jerked his shoulder away from her touch as if her skin were on fire. "Sorry," she whispered, dropping her arm to her side. She waited.

He turned to face her. He forced a thin smile on his lips. "I'm sorry; it's just my wife..." His voice trailed off and his next words caught in his throat.

"I'm sorry, I didn't know you were married." She sensed his sadness. "Did something happen to her?"

Phillip's watery gaze locked with hers. "No. Not really. She lives in Alaska. With my ex-partner."

Amanda wondered if maybe she'd trod on forbidden ground. "Sorry. It's none of my business. I—"

"It's OK, Miss Dark. Your empathy is a gift. Yes, I know about your ability to sense feelings. I wondered if it were true when I hired you. I can see it is, maybe a little too true."

Amanda raised both eyebrows. "What do you mean?"

"My wife left me ten years ago. We were high school sweethearts, but after our marriage it became clear our lives were on different paths. I still care about Julie, but we've both moved on."

Testing of her abilities was expected so Amanda wasn't insulted or annoyed. Honestly, if she were in a client's shoes, she would doubt as well. When you say it out aloud, a woman who chases ghosts for a living sounds like rubber room time. "Are you married now?" She winced. "Sorry, that's really none of my business."

Phillip laughed. "No worries. I'm just glad you're here." He arched an eyebrow. "And no, I'm not married. Divorced."

Time to change the subject. "Did you see a cat?"

The sexy smile disappeared from Phillip's features. He frowned. "Cat? Was it black, with a white-tipped tale?" Amanda nodded. "And did it disappear out this window?" He pointed to the window. "Or through a wall?"

Amanda's eyes widened. "How did you know?"

Phillip shrugged. "Come with me into the old library."

Amanda followed him out of the bedroom into a wide, musty hallway. They walked side by side to the end of the hall, where there were double doors. The original brass handles were now black with age and lay on the floor where they had fallen as the doors rotted away.

Phillip pushed the doors open and they went in. The old library walls were covered in shelves of rotting books. The odor of decay was heavy in the air. At one end of room sat a large, grandly carved oak desk. On the desk was a hand-carved wooden box, about the size of a modern briefcase. Only it clearly wasn't modern. The carvings depicted slaves harvesting tobacco leaves and a sailing vessel with its sails bulging from the wind. There was also a grinning skull over crossed swords, a classic motif for flags of the pirate age.

Amanda concluded that the box had once been the property of one Captain Blackblood Swann, Phillip's ancestor. Her eyes flitted to Phillip, then back to the box. Phillip certainly didn't look like a bloodthirsty pirate, or like any of the ugly pirates in those Disney movies. Actually, he looked more like the pirates adorning the covers of steamy romance novels.

A sun-warmed face turned nut brown, dark curls, and muscular arms clearly visible beneath his denim shirt, the top two buttons of which were undone to reveal a wisp of dark hair. His looks alone stirred her more than any man had in a long time.

Phillip moved to the desk and flipped open the lid of the box to reveal a well-worn, leather-bound book inside. A strong smell of leather filled the room. He gingerly lifted the book from the box and set it flat on the desk. Carefully, as if handling the Dead Sea Scrolls, he turned the yellowed pages to the middle of the thick volume.

Amanda stepped closer to study the odd writing. The words were written in the style of calligraphy, the writing ornate and flowing. "What is it?" she asked.

"The diary of Captain Henry Swann."

Amanda's eyes widened. "Really? "

He nodded. "The pages are brittle with age, so after we find the treasure, I plan to donate the book to the Smithsonian."

Treasure? A frown creased Amanda's brow. *I nearly kill myself, and the life-and-death mission I'm on is to help him find gold and silver?* Amanda wasn't rich; in fact, she was on the low side of the middle class, but she wasn't a treasure hunter. To her, contact with paranormal phenomena wasn't about seeking lost objects or obscene wealth, it was to help the dead achieve their just reward, or at least be released from earth to go on their way. Sometimes they didn't appreciate her intervention, but the living relatives often did.

"What's this about treasure?" she asked, straining to keep the anger in her gut from her tone.

Phillip swiveled to face her. He offered her a lopsided grin. "Sorry. I'm not a treasure hunter, if that's what you're thinking. No, I'm after something much more personal."

Amanda eyed him quizzically with one eyebrow cocked. Did he have her ability to sense emotions too? "What does his diary say?"

Phillip's shifted back to gaze down at the pages of the open book. "Captain Swann's diary says he had a cat. A black cat with a white-tipped tail. Its name was Scars."

Amanda's eyes went wide and she stepped to his side, her eyes on the pages. "Really? I saw a cat like that in my room..." Her cheeks grew warm. "Uh, I mean your room...uh...I mean the bedroom." *Oh, crap, he's gonna think I'm an idiot.* All she wanted to do right now was crawl into a dark corner and die of embarrassment.

Phillip, however, didn't seem to notice her sudden discomfort. His eyes were on the pages of the book. "Yes, I expect you saw the ghost of his cat."

Amanda shivered as a sudden coldness enveloped her, accompanied by a feeling of dread. She'd experienced feelings like these before, during investigations in haunted houses, but never with this intensity. Her heart beat hard and time seemed to slow down.

A sharp movement at the edge of her left eye made her turn her head slightly in that direction. What she saw made her freeze and draw in a ragged breath. Her heart beat rapidly. A man—dressed in pirate garb, with a long saber dangling from his belt, his dark eyes scowling at her, his white, frilly shirt stained with dirt—stood eyeing her with one hand resting on the hilt of the sword. His free arm cradled the cat she'd seen earlier, its white-tipped tail flicking to and fro. Could it be a hallucination caused by the blow to the head?

"Uh, Phillip, do you see him?"

Phillip looked at her, his eyes quizzical. "Who?"

Amanda pointed to where the pirate, with his three-cornered, wide-brimmed hat sporting a black feather, stood silently watching them.

Phillip scanned the spot she was pointing to and shook his head.

"I don't see anything..." His words trailed off and his face became the color of ash. "A ghost," he whispered. His hands were trembling. "You see a ghost, don't you?"

"Yes. At least, I think I do."

"You mean you've never seen one before?"

Amanda swallowed hard as she placed one hand on his arm. She needed to steady herself before she collapsed. Any second her knees would buckle and she'd drop to the floor. "As strange as it sounds, no, I've never seen a live one...uh, I mean a dead one..." Her mouth clamped shut to stop herself before she shoved both feet into it.

"What's he look like?"

Amanda shifted her gaze to the pirate, who eyed her curiously. He carried the cat to a chair across the room and sat down, now petting the cat with his other hand. The cat curled its tail lazily around its body and looked very content. Its unblinking, mustard-yellow eyes watched her.

"Well, he's a pirate and he has a cat. He's sitting on the chair—"

"Sorry to interrupt, Amanda, but there aren't any chairs in here. Haven't been in about two hundred years."

"Actually, he's sitting on one right over there..." Amanda nodded to the spot where the pirate sat watching her. He wore a half smile now. Amanda's fear had dissipated, replaced by growing annoyance. He was laughing at her. She was the only one who could see him and he found her predicament funny. Although truthfully, she'd find her hard to believe, too.

"Listen, Phillip, if I tell you there's a pirate over there sitting on a chair, then there is. I never lie. I don't know why I see him or his cat, and he may be the first ghost I've seen in the fles—in person, but I am a paranormal investigator. It's my job. It's what I do."

She wasn't sure the pirate was real, but she wasn't about to let anyone think badly of her chosen profession. Too many people thought paranormal investigators were scam artists and charlatans. Until they needed her services.

Phillip held up his hands in mock surrender. "OK, OK, I did check you out. I know you're a paranormal investigator, and according to my sources, you're a darned good one."

Amanda took a step away from him and eyed him with a scowl marring her forehead. "You checked me out. With whom?"

Phillip dropped his arms to his sides, rolled his eyes, and emitted a soft chuckle. "Trust me, Amanda, it's nothing untoward, I assure you. I'm a lawyer in Boston, where you also live, and I have a client who used your unique services a couple of years back. Do you remember Ollie Hardson?"

She did indeed remember Ollie, the man she'd dubbed the roamer because his hands often ended up in the wrong places—like on her bottom—at the most inappropriate times. She also recalled helping him remove the ghost of his dead Aunt Grace from his ancestral home. Of course, he then sold the old house to a developer for a small fortune. It's a strip mall now.

"You know Ollie?" she said.

Phillip snorted. "Yeah. Real creep." He shook his head. "I did the legal work on the sale of the house you cleared of his aunt's ghost. He told me all about it." He chuckled. "Never seen a guy so scared in all my life. His story reminded me of the ghost stories we used to tell around the fire at Camp Wobegon when I was a kid. But if there was one thing about Ollie, he convinced me the tale wasn't fantasy."

Maybe Phillip wasn't such a bad guy. If he was telling the truth. "Why don't you tell me what this is really all about?"

Phillip glanced at the watch on his left wrist. "I imagine you're hungry. Why don't we eat and I'll tell you all about it? And then if you don't want to help me, fine—you can keep the money and I'll call for a boat to take you back to Isle of Palms, no questions asked. Deal?"

Amanda considered his words. Phillip Swann was growing on her. And he seemed trustworthy, for a lawyer. She nodded. "Deal." Her stomach rumbled. She looked at Phillip, her eyes wide with horror. He laughed first, then she joined in.

Before they left the library, Amanda stole a quick glance at Captain Swann, who was still seated with Scars curled in his lap. He nodded when she walked passed him. His expression was pleasant. A pleasant pirate, who woulda thought?

**

Phillip surprised her when they went out the back door off the kitchen of the old house. The kitchen was beyond repair. Every wooden surface was cracked by wind and heat and the glass in the window frames here, too, were absent, so there was nothing to keep out the inclement weather when winter storms brushed the island. Phillip explained that the family home had been abandoned just prior to the Civil War. Parts of the house had been damaged when the Confederate army used the house as a headquarters from which to launch troops or ships against Union forces. In an attempt to drive out the rebel army, the Union navy had bombarded the island just as they had nearby Fort Sumter, but never succeeded in dislodging the Confederate troops.

At the rear of the house, Phillip had erected a tent, and to create his own shaded area, he'd tied the corners of a tarp to the trees ringing his campsite. In the center of the camp was a fire pit, a shallow pit dug in the soft sand and clay, ringed by large, smoke-blackened rocks. A stainless steel grate covered the pit. Off a tripod over the pit hung a steel hook holding an old-fashioned cast-iron cooking pot.

"Water?" Phillip asked, waving her to a camp chair to the right of the fire pit.

She nodded and sat in the chair. The air was rife with wood smoke. To the left of the tent was a pile of firewood.

He went to an orange cooler and took out two bottles of water, one of which he handed to her before squatting next to the pit and lighting the fire. Soon a blue-and-yellow flame danced under the grate, the wood snapping and popping as the moisture in the wood was heated and expelled. A trail of white smoke disappeared into the sky overhead.

Amanda broke the seal on the bottle and twisted off the cap. After taking a long swig of the cool water, she put the cap back on the bottle and placed it in her lap. "You seem to have been here for a while."

Phillip was concentrating on nursing the growing fire. "Yeah," he said, "a while. I was waiting for you. I sent the letter ago." He shrugged. "I didn't know how long it would take, so I may have over-prepared."

The fire crackled brightly and the flames now licked the grate. Satisfied, Phillip rose to his feet and moved to the cooler again. "Hot dogs OK?"

Since tubes of mystery meat were one of her favorite food groups,

Amanda readily agreed, but just as she did at home, she promised herself to eat better in future.

He glanced at her and grinned. "Good. Mustard, ketchup?"

Again she nodded.

Soon they were eating grilled hot dogs in silence, the smoke from the fire permeating everything.

Amanda swallowed a bite of meat, bun, and the mustard-ketchup mixture. She broke the silence first. "What's the treasure that you're so interested in if it's not gold and jewels?"

Phillip stopped eating and looked at her. His eyes were serious; she worried she may have offended him. "I'm hoping the chest buried somewhere on this island holds the truth about my famous ancestor."

Her curiosity aroused, Amanda continued. "I gather there is a letter or document that will tell a different story about Captain Swann than the tales told in the history books?"

Phillip took a small bite of his hot dog and nodded. "Yes. I believe there is a letter signed by Queen Anne of England, affirming that Captain Swann was an agent of the Queen in the Caribbean, raiding Spanish and French colonies and their ships to disrupt trade."

"That's very different than what's recorded about your ancestor." Amanda frowned. "Why is this so important to you now? Surely after three hundred years, it doesn't really matter all that much, does it?"

Phillip's face became a mask of determination, his jawline taut. He threw the remainder of his meal into the fire. The fatty meat flared and she could smell it charring. "Before my father died of cancer last year, he made me promise to clear the Swann name." He stopped and looked into her eyes. She watched his eyes lose their hard edge and his shoulders relax.

"Sorry. I must seem a little obsessed. I may be, but Dad always felt the reason Captain Swann's name was dishonored involved family land claims in England."

"Land claims?"

"Yes. When Queen Anne died in 1714, King Charles I assumed the throne. He was German and had little interest in English affairs of state; those he left to Sir Robert Walpole. The Walpoles and the Swanns were not on the best of terms since the Walpoles wanted the Swann lands, and because of a love affair that ended badly between cousins from each family."

Sounds like Romeo and Juliet, thought Amanda. She took a bite of her hot dog, chewed, and swallowed. "They didn't like each other. So what does this all have to do with Queen Anne's letter?"

Phillip shook his head. "Walpole had all copies of the letter destroyed and announced that the English navy would hunt down Captain Swann and hang him as a pirate, which they did in 1719. My grandfather told me something Walpole didn't know was that a single copy of Queen Anne's letter with the royal seal remained hidden on this island. Over the years, we've tried many times to find it without success."

Amanda finished her meal and felt rejuvenated. She took a sip of water, then said, "You want me to ask Captain Swann where the chest is hidden. Correct?"

"Yes."

"And I suppose there are jewels and gold buried with the document."

Phillip smiled. "I don't know. And frankly, I don't care."

"But I do," said a deep male voice to Amanda's left. Looking to the row of trees where the voice came from, she saw a tall, dark-skinned man step out from behind a tree. Her heart froze.

In his right hand he held a snub-nosed pistol pointed at them.

Phillip chuckled. "Ah, yes, Jim Sweet, my former partner. How nice of you to drop by. How long have you been listening?"

The corner of Sweet's mouth curled up. "Long enough to know you may have found the key to finding the treasure." He waved the gun at Amanda. "Her."

Phillip made a move to stand, but Sweet waved the pistol at him. "Don't move," Sweet said, his eyes narrowing.

Phillip's shoulders slumped and he remained seated. "OK, Jim, you win. What do you want?"

"I want this little lady to accompany me inside the house, talk the ghost into telling me where the treasure is hidden, and then I'll be on my way."

Phillip arched an eyebrow. "What about me?"

"I was thinking I'd dispose of you first, but if the captain won't talk to me, I may still need you. So I'm going to tie you up and leave you here. If I need you, I'll come back for you. If not..." Jim left the rest to their imagination, not that it needed much imagination to see he was going to kill them both, regardless of what happened. As the pirates used to say, dead men tell no tales.

If there was a treasure buried with the letter about Captain Swann, it would be worth a fortune in today's money. People have killed for far less.

"You," Sweet pointed the pistol at Amanda, "find a rope and tie him up."

Amanda looked to Phillip. He nodded and pointed to the tent. "There's a rope inside."

Amanda's thoughts grew cold. They were going along with this man? *Why?*

Soon, after some instruction by Sweet, she had Phillip tied to the chair.

"Let's go," Sweet said, his voice menacing, his eyes flat with no emotion. How did Phillip get hooked up with such a man, someone capable of killing in cold blood?

Amanda started walking toward the house, followed by Sweet, who had the gun pressed into her back. One thing her father had insisted she learn before she left home to move to the big city was how to use and care for guns. She didn't really like guns, but when someone has one pressed into your spine, knowledge could come in handy. Six hours a week at a gun range for three months made a girl fairly proficient with firearms.

She entered the house and went immediately to the library, where they'd left the diary open on the weathered desk. Amanda was disappointed to see that the chair, Captain Swann, and his cat were missing.

Moving to the book, she pretended to read it. Her eyes flitted to movement as Sweet came from behind to stand beside her. He had the gun pointing to the floor at his side. He didn't see her as a threat.

A small smile played across Amanda's lips. Once his attention was on the book, she decided her opportunity would never be better, so she reached for the gun and managed to grab it and twist it out of his hand before he could react.

Stepping away, she raised the weapon and pointed it at Sweet's chest. A quick glance confirmed the safety was off.

Sweet regarded her with his dead eyes. "Go ahead," he said, "shoot." He took a step toward her and she instinctively took a step back.

One thing her father hadn't taught her was the killer instinct. Shooting paper targets was very different from shooting a living person. Her fingers gripping the pistol began to sweat. "Don't move," she said.

"I don't think you'll fire," said Sweet, stepping closer. He raised one hand and slowly reached for the gun.

"Don't! I will, you know..."

Sweet grabbed the barrel of the pistol and pulled it from her slick fingers. Amanda's heart sank. She'd failed both herself and Phillip. They were going to die.

Sweet smiled grimly. "Now stop this nonsense and talk to the ghost about the treasure." He pointed the gun at her forehead. "Right now," he growled, "or I will shoot you, and I won't chicken out."

"Sweet!" It was Phillip's voice. Suddenly Sweet and the pistol were no longer menacing her. At her feet lay the tangled mass of two men locked in combat.

Amanda backed up until her body was pressed against the wall, while watching the struggling men. Phillip landed a punch on Sweet's jaw, and Sweet's head snapped to the right. Bones crunched and she could see that Philip's knuckles were bleeding. Sweet grunted from another blow and his head snapped back. He raised the pistol, which miraculously he hadn't let go of when Phillip tackled him.

Gritting his teeth, Phillip grabbed Sweet's arm and twisted it hard backward, causing the pistol to fly out of his hand. The gun struck the wall behind them with a thud, then rattled to the floor. Amanda considered going for the weapon, but if she tried, the two fighting men might knock her to the floor. The room was too small for her to maneuver around them. They leaped to their feet and circled each other warily.

Sweet's eyes kept flicking from Phillip to the gun, then back again. Phillip's attention was focused solely on his opponent.

Sweet's hands formed fists. He rushed forward and swung a fist at Phillip's head. Phillip ducked inside Sweet's intended blow and landed a hard blow to Sweet's solar plexus.

The air rushed from Sweet's lungs; he gasped, clutching his belly as he stumbled backward. Phillip stepped forward, landed a punch hard on Sweet's chin. The man's head snapped around and he collapsed into a heap on the floor where he lay still, his eyes closed. It was over. Phillip had won.

Phillip moved unsteadily on rubbery legs. His lip was bleeding. His left cheek sported a purple bruise that was already badly swollen. He dragged air into his lungs.

Amanda rushed to him. She wrapped her arms around him, partially to keep him from falling and partially to comfort him. She grasped his shoulders and studied his bloodshot eyes. "Phillip, thank you for saving me."

He gave her a weak smile. "No worries."

"Who is he?" She nodded toward Sweet, lying unconscious on the floor.

"My former law partner," Phillip said.

Amanda's eyes went wide. "He's a lawyer? Would he really have killed us?"

"Oh, yes. Jim Sweet was convicted of murdering his wife and his mother-in-law. And that was for one hundred thousand dollars in insurance money. A priceless treasure proved too much for a greedy creep like him." His eyes drooped at the corners. "I should never have told him about my ancestor, but I thought he was my friend."

They quickly tied Sweet's hands and feet so he would be unable to move once he regained consciousness.

A cold dread washed over her, sending chills up her spine. Maybe it was emanating from Sweet or Phillip, but she didn't think so. She released Phillip and he leaned against the wall and watched her as she moved to the desk and opened the diary again. She looked back to the spot where she'd seen the pirate before. Sure enough, there he was—seated, as before, on the chair, with the cat in his lap.

"Hello, lass," he said. There was definitely an English inflection in his voice.

Amanda thought for a second or two that she might faint. Not only had she seen her first ghost, but he'd just spoken to her.

"Uh...hello?"

Phillip frowned. "Who are you talking to?"

"He's here again."

"Oh. Quick, before he leaves again, ask him where the treasure is hidden."

Amanda opened her mouth to speak, but the ghost rose from the chair, his hand resting on the hilt of his sword. The cat dropped to all fours, its tail waving back and forth.

"Why should I tell you that?" the ghost said.

"Is something wrong?" asked Phillip.

This go-between conversation could get complicated. She had to discover another way to get these two together. "Captain. I'm wondering if you will show yourself to Phillip." She indicated Phillip with a slight nod of her head.

The ghost scowled. He didn't appear open to the idea.

Perhaps if she shared some information about Phillip, the captain might be more agreeable.

"Captain. I'd like to introduce you to your great-great-great-grandson, Phillip Swann."

Hook Island

The ghost arched one eyebrow. She'd tweaked his interest, but not secured his cooperation. Time to go for broke. She wondered if ghosts had traces of their human emotions remaining. She hoped so. If not, then this would fall flatter than the soufflé she had tried to make once in Life Skills class. "Before Phillip's father died, he asked Phillip to clear his family name."

The ghost's eyebrows rose together and his dark eyes narrowed. "What trickery be this, lass? I am charged by the Queen herself to be her agent in these waters."

"That was three hundred years ago. You were betrayed by Lord Walpole, who branded you as a pirate and had you hung in 1719."

The ghost of Captain Swann ran one hand across his throat. She knew she'd triggered a buried memory, and not a pleasant one. She continued her explanation. "Lord Walpole had all copies of the letter destroyed except the one you hid here on the island. In order to clear your name in the history books, we need that letter."

Captain Swann frowned, then said, "OK, lass, the boy can see me now."

Amanda's eyes flicked to Phillip. His face was pale and his eyes wide. He indeed could see the pirate captain. She worried it might be too much for him, especially in his weakened condition. As she watched, his features relaxed and his demeanor changed. His face became calm and his eyes reflected determination. "Captain Swann. Sir. I'm your great-great-great-grandson, Phillip—"

The ghost captain interrupted him with a burst of laughter, his features now split by a wide grin. "Weren't ya listen to the lass here, boyo? She told me yor tale of woe. Or should ah say my tale of woe."

Phillip's eyes flitted to Amanda and his cheeks flushed crimson. "Yes, of course." He smiled weakly at her.

36

"She's a special lady, with special powers."

"Lad, if ya press the palm of yor hand six inches to the right of that corner," he gestured to one corner of the room, "where the two walls meet, a hidden panel will open. Inside, you will find the letter from mah Queen." With those words the captain faded, then disappeared. Looking around, Amanda saw that Scars the cat had also disappeared.

"Wow. That was something," said Phillip, expelling the breath he'd been holding in. "Do you still see him?" he asked, looking at Amanda.

She shook her head. "Let's see what's hidden in the wall," she suggested.

Phillip moved to the corner and pressed the wall as the ghost had instructed. There was a soft click, then, as if it were on a hinge, a portion of the wall from the floor to the ceiling swung inward. The section was no more than six inches wide—not enough to hide a treasure chest, that much was clear. Dust accompanied the panel opening. Amanda sneezed when the dust filled her nose.

"Bless you," said Phillip. He reached into the open panel and pulled out a four-foot-long, tube-shaped leather case. It had a carrying strap on one side, and the size and shape suggested it might contain a map.

Amanda's heart beat rapidly; she was anxious to see what was inside. Phillip carried it to the desk. She followed. They stood side by side as he opened the top of the case and peered inside. A smile played across his lips, then became a full blown grin.

"I see a document inside."

"Is it a map?"

"Yes, tell us, Phil, is there a treasure map in there?"

Amanda froze and shut her eyes tightly. *Oh, crap, Sweet's awake. How did he untie the ropes?* A soft click told her whoever it was had the pistol. They were right back where they had started. Doomed.

"Well, well, ya scurvy dog, do ya think I'd let the likes o' you get the drop on me family?"

A bloodcurdling scream made the hair on the back of her neck stand at attention and sent shivers down her spine. The scream ended abruptly, as if a tap had been turned off. Amanda opened one eye to steal a look at Phillip. He, too, had his eyes shut.

After several seconds of silence that seemed like an eternity, Amanda decided to take a look. She opened her eyes and turned around.

There was no sign of Sweet, the captain, or his cat. All that remained was the pistol, lying on the floor, resting near the wall where their would-be murderer must have dropped it. She tapped Phillip on his shoulder. He turned around.

"What happened?" he asked.

Amanda shook her head slowly. "I have no idea. I've never known ghosts to interact with the living. Unless..." It couldn't be, but it was the only sane explanation, if you could call the paranormal sane. She set her jaw and explained. "I've read about this, but have never met anyone who's seen it. At least, anyone who's still alive."

Phillip looked at her in awe, his eyes wide. She continued. "In 1891, a man named Simon Polson, a medium reputed to have been to the other side, reported that when ghosts feel threatened or when they're angered they can will themselves to touch and interact physically with the real world. Polson said it drained them and in some cases destroyed them, but if the ghost were powerful enough, they could even drag the living into the spirit world.

The living would not be able to escape and would spend eternity neither living nor dead, in limbo."

Phillip shuddered. "Sounds horrible. Do you think that's what happened to Jim?"

Amanda nodded. "Yes, I think so. But as my mother used to say, he made his bed, he has to lie in it."

She turned to the desk and picked up the map case. "If this is the letter, then we need to take it to a museum to get it authenticated. Old documents will crumble unless they're treated with great care. Do you agree?"

"Yes, but I'm anxious to see the letter."

Amanda grinned. "Me as well, but we have to be patient."

Phillip offered her a lopsided grin, which got her juices flowing again. "Perhaps you and I can work together once we get back to Boston. What do you think?"

Amanda wanted to see him again in the worst way possible. Or was it the best? She smiled to herself. "Well, Mr. Swann, I think we can arrange something, but since you saved my life, I must insist you let me buy you dinner."

"Agreed." He held out his hand, she took it in hers, and shook to seal their agreement. Reluctantly she let go.

"Let's pack up your camp and call for a boat. I'm sure Pierre wouldn't mind coming back for us," she said.

Phillip nodded, then took the leather case from her and walked out of the library into the hall.

A small movement to her left shifted her attention from the doorway toward the wall. Scars appeared, padded to her, and rubbed his body against her legs, emitting a gentle purring sound. She sighed. Not only did she have a new friend and business partner, but somehow she had adopted a ghost cat.

Amanda watched Phillip go and it dawned on her that her life was headed on a new path. She might even have discovered a best friend, and maybe more.

Hopefully much more.

Rita Schulz is an accomplished romance author who writes in various genres. Her western romance published by Champagne Books is titled Fire in Their Hearts *and is written under the name Rita Meger. She has published numerous short stories and collections with 53rd Street Publishing and we are proud to include this scary coming-of-age tale in this volume.*

Silver Light

Rita Schulz

JANET SWIFT, A TALL YOUNG WOMAN, picked up the antique brush from the top of the rosewood dresser and stared at herself in the mirror. Her slender form was bathed in the silver light of the moon coming through the window overlooking the rambling, colorful gardens below.

More than any other room in the house, she loved this one in her grandparents' rustic two-story farmhouse at the edge of the urban sprawl that the metropolis of Vancouver had become. Their welcoming home had an expansive front porch painted hunter green with a rich, warm white trim.

Her favorite thing had always been her room, her safe haven after her parents died when she was six. Being here had helped her heal from the grief of losing both parents at the same time.

This old house, with its creaky oak floors and its large airy rooms, was what she always thought of as her real home.

Silver Light

The house had been updated in the last year, but her room was the same as when she lived here two years ago. She still came home to visit all the time and knew she was very lucky her grandparents were a big part of her life.

In three days' time she would change; she would be married and never be the same person again. Thoughts of her impending wedding made her palms sweat and her mouth go dry.

Her grandparents really liked Richard, her fiancé, and had given their blessing to the marriage.

As Janet stood, she swayed back and forth to music only she could hear. It was the song the orchestra would play at her wedding.

She froze when she thought she heard the well-oiled lock on her door click to lock her in. *I must still be dreaming*, she concluded.

Even the hairbrush felt strange as it ran though her hair. She stopped, then made another stroke and stopped again. She looked down at the floor and her breath caught in her throat. Her hair. Her long, silky, beautiful blond hair rained down silently around her shoulders as it fell to the floor in chunks.

Her eyes grew wide and her heart beat hard. She leaned forward to stare at her image in the mirror. *What's happening to me?*

Her hair was nearly gone now, only stubbles separated her from complete baldness. What was left was coarse, dense, sandy-colored, and barely two inches long. The brush slipped from her fingers as her hands moved to the top of her head. She emitted a scream, then screamed again.

Her heart raced as her mind tried to grasp what she was seeing. She turned, ran to the bedroom door. She had to get out. The crystal doorknob turned in her hand but the door wouldn't open. It was locked.

Janet shook the knob and pounded on the door.

It wouldn't open. She screamed again and again as she pounded on the door with a closed fist. Her voice grew hoarse, but no one came. Her mind whirled with fear and confusion.

This door was never locked. Where were her grandparents?

Finally she managed to calm herself. It was a nightmare, just a nightmare. It was the same nightmare she'd had for the last two weeks.

She'd had nightmares since she was a little girl but had learned how to control, or at least manage, them. This was nothing more than a bad dream that couldn't hurt her. It had to be.

As she walked back to the bed, she started her calming exercises. Controlling her breathing and racing heart, she lay on her back on her bed. The bed sighed as she sat and seemed to gently accept her body as she lay back on the soft mattress. All she needed was to do a few of the relaxation techniques she's learned from her psychologist.

Janet closed her eyes and breathed deeply in through her nose and then out through her mouth. Each breath she held for two seconds before she let it out. Ten times. Done.

Her heartbeat finally returned to normal. She opened her eyes. The room looked just like the bedroom she'd had when she had been a little girl, but small things had been changed that she hadn't noticed before.

The only thing that made sense was she was still asleep and these events must be part of her on-going nightmare, but this time it was taking a different twist. Her heart rate increased as her breathing once again became rapid. *No*, she thought, *I can't let this happen.*

Janet tried relaxing again. It was working. Her heart was slowing and her breath was becoming even and deep.

Her eyes opened. She was still in the same bedroom.

She sat up and slipped off the bed, then went to the door.

Silver Light

She turned the knob but it still wouldn't open. This time she also noticed the door's hinges were outside the room. Someone had changed the door.

She walked to the large bedroom window. It was a beautiful window, with new white steel filigree bars. She gripped the bars tightly and pulled; they didn't give at all. She pulled again, as hard as she could. The entire casement was steel. It was solid.

The room was pretty, but now she knew that there were bars on the window and a locked door. It was no longer a safe haven, it had become a very strong prison and she was locked in it.

She had to get out. There had to be something she could use to pry the door or the window open or, at the very least, a weapon to use against whoever had her locked in. Her jaw tightened. Whoever it was would pay for locking her in this cage.

She checked the closets first. There were only clothes hung on wooden hangars. She next went to the four-drawer pine dresser set against the wall at the end of the bed. Opening a drawer, she smiled when she discovered her black leather hobo purse. She grabbed the purse and carried it to the bed. Opening it, she rummaged inside for her cell phone. It was missing.

There was nothing in the purse that could help her contact anyone or protect herself. No nail file, not even a pencil or pen; they had all been removed. Someone had been very clever.

The rustle of the wind brushing the light blue curtains on either side of the window drew her attention. Janet went to the open window to look at the night sky. She looked at the thin clouds scuttling across the face of the large silver moon high on the horizon. She pressed her face to the bars in the window and gulped the cool crisp air into her lungs. Then greedily she sniffed the night air carried by the breeze.

So many wonderful scents: jasmine, honeysuckle, and roses. The fresh wind felt so much better than the stuffy air of the bedroom.

A sudden tingling in her fingers made her look at her hands. They looked the same, only her fingers seemed a little longer, thinner. Maybe her nails were thicker and stronger. *Am I still dreaming?*

She walked to the mirror to again look at herself. The woman looking back at her was no more than twenty-five and in good physical shape. Her blonde hair was now only two to three inches long; it looked as if she had gotten a chunky cut.

How could she appear like this at her wedding? She was a freak. Her eyes filled with tears and a lump formed in her throat. Janet knew she had bigger problems right now. her grandparents were somehow at the epicenter. Her emotions whirled through her mind, sadness mingled with fear, then anger...*why is this happening to me?*

Maybe her grandparents had gone crazy, off their rockers; could that even happen to two people at the same time? *All this time I thought they loved me. Could I be wrong?*

She leaned closer to the mirror and gazed into her eyes. Her light brown eyes had taken on a golden appearance, flecked with copper. It occurred to her she was looking at her grandfather's eyes.

OK, the hair looked thicker, the fingers a little different too, maybe the shape of her face? Was that different as well? She leaned forward and peered into the mirror. The light wasn't the best in this room right now.

Janet sat down on the edge of her bed and looked around the room carefully, trying to remember how it had looked before today. She decided she must be imagining things. Or was she?

She needed, really needed, to get out of this room. A deep fear suddenly gnawed at her belly. She rose to her feet and started pacing.

She kept pushing the thought that she couldn't get out of the room to the back of her mind. She was afraid if she let herself consider this situation might be permanent, she would lose control and never regain it. She could feel herself begin to tremble and then shake.

She thought she heard a sound from below and quickly moved to the door.

"Nona, are you there? Is Opa with you?" Janet called out, making sure she remained calm and didn't yell. Her grandparents hated raised voices.

"Please, it's Janet." Her voice echoed off the walls around her and she strained to detect a response. There was none. She strangled the scream in her throat and continued on gently. "I know I haven't visited very much in the last month or two, and I should call more, but this is a little extreme. Could you please let me out?"

Janet waited. She pressed her ear to the door and listened intently for a sound, any sound at all.

Nothing.

Then she heard the faint sound of the kitchen clock ticking downstairs. The old wooden stairway groaned and the old oak floors moaned. Normal sounds for this old house. She'd always felt safe when she heard the house move and breathe around her.

Janet moved to the bedroom window again and took in a lungful of air. It was dark now and her stomach rumbled from hunger. It sure sounded like her gut was empty. She wondered how long she had been here. Maybe they had knocked her out?

The last thing she really remembered was talking to her best friend and bridesmaid, Susan, about the details of her impending wedding. They had been in Janet's apartment. After Susan was gone, she had heard a noise on her balcony. Odd.

It was the last thing she could recall. She had no memory of driving to her grandparents' house at all.

Janet had taken three days off work before the wedding, and two weeks' vacation after for the honeymoon.

She tried to understand what was happening to her and why. A deep sense of panic rose from within her. Her breathing grew rapid again.

Sitting down on her bed, she smoothed the down quilt with one hand. It was soft and the smell reminded her of the fresh scent of the outdoors. That meant Nona had hung it outside to air out.

If she was at her grandparents' and they weren't here, then they would be back soon. Maybe Nona was getting the fixings to make her a special breakfast, just like on her birthdays. She smiled to herself and her pulse rate finally slowed and her stomach settled. They probably just wanted her to themselves for a day or so before the wedding.

Her brow wrinkled. But why was her door locked?

What if they had been hurt? What if all this was a plot by kidnappers?

She shook off the feeling of confusion and doubt. Nerves, it was just nerves that were making her so spooked.

Janet walked over to the window again. The hardwood floors were cool now under her bare feet. She looked longingly at the old double garage. Her grandparents always parked their car on the left of the solid wood structure. There were windows on the right side of where Opa's workshop and Nona's potting shed were. But this wasn't helping her get out. Right now Janet didn't care about the garage. A feeling of anxiousness rose in her again. She wiped her sweaty palms on her nightgown.

Silver Light

For the first time since waking, she really looked at the nightgown she wore. She had never seen it before. Where had it come from and who had put it on her? The short hair on the back of her neck stood up and she shivered.

The longer she thought, the more questions she had. She hated unanswered questions. She liked things tidy, orderly. She was overly curious by nature. The questions she had in her mind were going to make for some very interesting discussions with her grandparents.

Janet clenched her fists, her nails digging into her palms like knives. Her nails, which she always wore very short, were now digging into her palms. Relaxing her hands, she stared at them. Her nails had grown thick, sharp, and curved. She smiled as a sense of satisfaction washed over her; she could do some serious damage with these babies.

A dog howled from somewhere down the street. From deep in her throat she snarled. With all the strength she could manage, she fought the urge to lift her head and howl with the dog. It seemed a joyful noise. The dog was serenading the moon and calling to friends to join in with him.

The wind rustled the branches in the trees. Sounds and scents, everything seemed to be amplified. A familiar sound met her ears. Her grandparents' car was coming down the driveway.

She waited and watched the car from her window.

The breeze and the branches from the tall cherry tree created shifting shadows on the roof of the garage. She knew she could easily climb from the tree onto the roof. Then she could chase the shadows on the roof and play in the tall grasses at the base of the tree. The real question would be which to do first? She smiled at the thought of chasing shadows and playing.

Rita Schulz

Janet was losing control and that had never happened to her before. She always maintained ridged control. A two drink maximum and no drugs, even prescription ones. She hated the feeling of losing control, of not being in charge. It scared her. She was terrified if she ever lost control she would never be able to regain it again. That it would be the end of her, she would disappear completely.

She started to shake and pulled her mind back to her grandparents as she watched the car's interior light come on as the driver's side door open and her grandfather got out.

She called to him through the open window, causing Opa to look up at her and wave. He walked around the hood of the car and opened the door for Nona. When her grandmother got out, they both looked up at the window, their lips formed thin straight lines, and they both waved at her.

Why didn't they seem to find it strange she was here? She had always had a key to their house, but had never used it. After all, they lived fairly close together.

A shadow passed over the window. She looked up at the sky in time to see broken clouds again pass in front of the silvery moon. Pretty.

She realized her reaction to everyday things was very strange. Now it seemed that the moon was for howling at, shadows on the roof tempted her to climb up the tree to chase them, but she couldn't.

She watched her grandparents move to the back of the car, then retrieve a couple of green cloth shopping bags.

They had a lot of explaining to do.

"Hey! I'm locked in the bedroom," she yelled from the window. "Let me out."

Nona's head turned and she looked up at Opa. Janet noticed their backs were turned to her.

At this distance she couldn't make out what they were saying very well, but she tried anyway. She cleared her mind and focused. As she concentrated, she thought she could make out a few words.

Losing focus, her mind slipped to the wedding plans. Would people like the red velvet wedding cake? She had to focus on what was happening here and she dragged her mind back to what was being said outside.

Closing her eyes, she concentrated again. She heard a few words, then bits of phrases. "Doesn't know…how long? Maybe she's not a…"

"Come on, will you? Please. I need to use the bathroom," she called out of the window. OK it wasn't the greatest ploy, but it should work.

Nona looked up and nodded to her as she led the way to the back door, with Opa following her.

Janet's words about the bathroom were true. Her bladder screamed for relief.

Soon there were footsteps coming up the stairs from the main floor. She stood next to the door on the side with the doorknob. She planned on getting out of this room, and if her grandparents were in her way, well, she'd either go over, around, or through them. She was determined to get out.

She shifted her weight from one foot to the other, balancing on the balls of her feet.

A key rattled as it was inserted into the lock, then turned. As the door opened a crack, she sprang forward. The door slammed shut and her shoulder hit the door hard.

"What are you doing, Nona? Opa, what's going on? Someone get me out!" Her heart raced, her breath came in gasps.

"Child, still yourself. We're coming. William, are you ready?"

"Yes, dear, I just wanted to put the ice cream away first. She can't hurt anything," Opa said, after she heard his slow, heavy steps coming up the stairs.

"Why am I locked in here?"

"Janet. Move away from the door, don't try and rush us again," said Nona. "You'll just hurt your poor little shoulder again. I know you must feel very confused right now."

"Nona, what's going on?" Tears filled her eyes as she walked back to the bed. Then she turned, ran back, and stood by the side of the door.

Janet pressed her ear against the door and listened intently. She heard the key turn in the lock and watched the doorknob turn. This time she would wait until they opened it wider, then she would rush out. She'd spring past them, run down the stairs and out the front door. She could move faster than they could. She was young and in good shape while they were old and slow.

She heard a loud sigh. Taking a deep breath, she held it, then leaned her body forward ready to run.

The door opened to reveal Nona and a large red timber wolf standing to one side of the door.

Ignoring her surprise, Janet ran for all she was worth through the door—and flipped over the broom handle Nona was holding. Janet landed flat on her back, the wind knocked out of her.

A low, throaty growl made her look at the wolf. But it hadn't made the noise. She had been the one who growled.

"What the hell is going on?"

"It's all right, Janet. We'll explain everything," Nona said in a gentle, reassuring voice as a soft cloth covered Janet's nose and mouth.

Silver Light

Janet lifted her hands up to push the nasty smell away, but her eyes lost their focus as everything went dark.

***

"Would you like a cup of tea, dear?" Opa's warm, gruff voice made her smile. It made her remember all the stories he would tell her when she was little.

"Or maybe something cool to drink would be better?" Nona's voice was soft and light. Janet remembered all the wonderful stories and adventures that that voice would read to her.

Janet blinked but things around her were slightly out of focus. She recognized the kitchen of her grandparents' two-story farmhouse. OK, that was fine. She stared at the two people in front of her. These were her grandparents. At least they looked and sounded like them.

Janet blinked harder to clear her eyes and ease the fog still clouding her brain.

She tried to move her arms and legs and realized they were tied to one of the hard pine kitchen chairs.

Her heart started to race again as the moisture in her mouth evaporated. Fear gripped her. These people couldn't be her grandparents. Everything and everybody looked the same, but it wasn't the same, couldn't be.

This was her safe place with people who loved and protected her. Her hands were slick with sweat and her legs trembled.

"It's OK, Janet, breathe," urged Nona gently.

Janet took in a deep breath, then slowly let it out.

"How about some cool water?" Opa said as he came to stand next to her.

She looked up at him. It was Opa all right, not the tallest of men, but not the shortest either. He was strong, wiry, and had been as long as she'd known him.

"How do you want to do this?" Opa asked Nona.

"Just like we discussed. I think the show-and-tell method would work best."

Opa held the glass to Janet's lips and tipped it up slowly so she could drink. She sipped at first, realized how thirsty she was, and then tried to gulp it down. "OK, that's enough for now," he said, pulling it away.

"Janet, now watch me. You may be a little shocked, but we'll answer all your questions. OK?" Nona looked into Janet's eyes.

"Who are you people and what did you do with my grandparents? I demand you let me go, right now." Panic gripped Janet and her stomach muscles tightened.

Nona looked at Janet and gave her a tender half grin as she slipped off her sweater and slippers.

She walked a few feet from Janet, stopped, then started to change. First her eyes changed. They took on a deep gray color and the irises changed to the shape of a cat's eyes. Then her face changed shape as her hands and feet developed fur and claws. She dropped down on her hands and knees and soon slipped out of her clothes. Her body was now that of a beautiful, tawny mountain lion or cougar.

Janet was filled with a burst of joy. She wanted to reach out and touch the large cat. She had never seen such a beautiful animal.

Suddenly her brain was overwhelmed with terror by what she'd just witnessed. She screamed.

Janet jerked and tugged at her ropes, struggling to get free.

53

Her stomach heaved and she clenched her jaw tight trying to keep from vomiting. "What did you put in the water? You drugged me. Are you going to kill me? Why?"

Opa said nothing, he just offered a tight-lipped smile as his shoulders slumped. She started to scream hysterically.

"Janet. Stop that!" Nona ordered.

Janet was shocked by her grandmother's tone, but it had a ring of command she couldn't ignore.

"That's quite enough, young lady." Nona was sitting on the floor now, in human form and once again in her clothes.

Janet blinked her eyes. She must be seeing things. She was hallucinating. It was the stress from working too many hours. The wedding was so close and there remained so many things to do. That was it. She was just having a temporary mental meltdown.

"We'll explain everything. Calm down, child, don't hurt yourself." Opa sighed as he looked at Janet.

Janet had never seen her grandmother look so authoritative. Nona held her head high, her spine was straight, and her shoulders were square. She quickly stood up in one fluid motion, unlike the frail old woman she was.

"You think you're seeing things. Fine. We'll take this slowly. William, it's your turn."

"Are you sure…?"

"Now, William. Richard should be coming to visit soon. No, we're not going to eat him, Janet." Nona chuckled. "Sorry, just a little fairy-tale humor."

Janet sat there, her eyes darting from one to the other. *I'm safe. I'm safe. It's OK, I'm safe.*

Nona pulled up a chair, set it next to Janet's, then sat down.

54

"Now watch carefully and Opa is going to turn into a beautiful red timber wolf. He may even look familiar to you." Nona looked at Janet.

Opa took off his slippers, his shirt, and loosened his belt.

Then he changed, too. Nona was right, she did recognize him as the red German Shepherd that she used to play with.

"Nona, he's not a wolf, he's the German Shepherd that used to visit us."

"Yes, and those times were during the full moon," Nona said.

Opa, in the guise of the , padded into the hall, his clothing in his mouth.

"Oh, come on, you can't tell me this is real. I get it—it's a joke. Right?" Janet almost snorted, but she stopped when she heard the front doorbell ring.

Finally, Richard had arrived. He'd set her free. He had always been the levelheaded one.

"I'll get it," said Opa from the hall as he went to the front. She heard the door open. "Come on in, Richard, we're in the kitchen."

Soon a beautiful tan wolf with a thick black mane walked into the kitchen. His ears perked, then he lifted his muzzle and sniffed deeply. His head tipped to one side and his tail wagged from side to side when he looked at Janet.

"Hi, Richard, we're really glad you're here," said Nona to the wolf.

"I'm afraid she's not taking the news very well. We thought we had prepared her, but I guess we must have missed the mark entirely," Opa explained, entering the kitchen dressed and in his human form.

"Janet, this is Richard in his other form," said Opa.

The wolf sat on its haunches, its tongue lolled out of the side of its mouth. The animal emitted a soft woof.

"No, we tried that. We read her all the folk tales, fairy tales, and legends. She enjoyed them, or seemed to. I don't know why she's freaking out so badly now." Opa looked at Nona, who nodded, confirming what he said.

Janet watched as the wolf and Opa walked out into the hall again. Hushed voices drifted in through the open door, then a closet opened, then closed.

"We explained folk tales and fairy tales all have a grain of truth. We even explained everything to her again just last week. This is so frustrating. We weren't even sure she had the ability; after all, she's twenty-five years old now." Her grandfather's voice grew fainter as he moved down the hallway, but she could still hear him clearly.

"Look, Opa, I'm not twenty-five yet, not until next month," said Janet. "And what do you mean, you prepared me? What has this got to do with fairy tales and stuff?"

"Janet, do you know what fairy tales, stories, and legends have in common?" said a deep male voice she knew was Richard's. He'd come back into the kitchen, in human form and dressed.

How could he be part of this craziness?

Her grandparents were one thing; maybe they were just off their medication, but steady, levelheaded Richard? Her mind reeled, unable to process this madness.

If she could get the grands back on the right meds, they could put this all behind them; then the wedding would go on as planned.

The wedding was in days. She still had to finalize the last few details. That was what was important. Not some crazy fantasy of her grandparents.

What about Richard? How could she marry him now?

56

He was nuts, too. Her head was spinning.

"OK, Janet, sweetie. What are you thinking?" Richard came across the tiled kitchen floor toward her.

"I'm trying to decide if you being a wolf is a deal breaker to us being married."

"Are you crazy? You're worried about the wedding?" Richard reached out and took Janet's hand. She felt his rough calluses against her skin.

"Me? You're calling me crazy? What have you done to my grandparents?"

Janet was breathing hard and shaking. Her heart pounded and perspiration rolled down her forehead. She licked her dry lips.

This was her family, her grandparents, the people who loved her and raised her.

They protected her from the nightmares of creatures coming alive in fairy tales they had read to her and she had seen in the beautiful graphic novels they collected and shared with her.

If she were to accept this was real and let herself go, she knew what was left of her mind would shatter into millions of pieces.

"Janet, honey, I understand the first time you change can be scary, but you're with people who love you."

"Just relax, see the silver light, feel the pull," said Nona, whose palms were pressed together almost as if she were praying.

"Please, darling," said Opa. "Do we know yet if she's a shape shifter or a were?" he asked Nona.

Nona shook her head. "It doesn't matter. Right now we need to support her through her first change."

"What brought this on now?" asked Richard.

"Janet, once you change, you'll find it a release, freeing. Are you able to tell me what you're feeling right now?"

Nona stood in front of her, studying her.

Janet looked back at Nona. Janet's forehead was bathed in sweat. Her nails dug into her palms and she realized she was bleeding. The blood smelled good. She licked her lips. She'd love a nice, blood rare steak. Janet's stomach growled.

What's the matter with me? Crazy. I'm losing my mind. Janet took in a deep breath and tried to focus on what was happening inside herself.

"I'm focusing on the wedding. It is the only thing I can control even a little bit. Everything else that's happening is insane." Beads of sweat ran down Janet's face. To try to steady herself, she dragged in a deep, ragged breath.

Nona sat down cross-legged next to Janet. "You're right, of course. I'll give you the facts. Ready?"

Nona seemed calm and confident. Janet hoped she would get the truth about what was happening to her.

Janet nodded. "Go ahead. Please."

"I am a shape shifter, and I prefer the shape of a mountain lion. I'm from a long line of shifters. Your grandfather's a werewolf. Your father was normal. Your mother didn't show any signs of shifting. The ability to change sometimes skips generation. That's why we didn't know if you were going to have the gift or not"

"What happened to my parents, really? How did they die?" Finally, the million-dollar question she'd always wanted to ask about her parents. Now it was out in the open.

"Really. It was stormy, your father was driving, and as best we know, he took the turn just on the outside of town too fast." Opa recited the story they had always told her. But now Janet could hear his elevated heart rate and smell fear on him.

Janet looked at Nona. "I can't trust you unless you tell me the truth. What really happened?"

Nona sucked in a deep breath. "Look at me, Janet."

Janet lifted her eyes and met her grandmother's gaze. "Your mother. She was twenty-five and was unprepared. We are reasonably sure she turned into a wolf and killed your father. You were there at the time. And you were only five years old."

Janet's eyes glazed over. "I remember. The blood. The yelling and growling. The noise wouldn't stop."

Opa nodded. "We're not really sure."

Janet's eyes filled with tears, blurring her vision. "I know what happened. He'd had an affair. I remember her yelling; she could smell the other woman on him. He was leaving us and she couldn't allow it."

Janet's jaw thrust forward. She looked down and realized her feet were changing. They were turning into paws tipped with razor sharp claws.

"Janet, I love you. Now I need you to relax. We'll help you." Richard walked behind her and untied her wrists while Opa untied her ankles. She slid onto the floor and lay on her back.

Years of unexplained feelings and nightmares finally made sense.

Janet knew she had to lose control to find out who she really was. She looked up at them and relaxed her body. Maybe all this wasn't her imagination. Maybe it was something much more terrifying, but she had to find out.

She smiled as she freed her mind. Her body began to reshape itself.

At last the truth set her free in the silver light of the moon.

Every collection of horror must have a magic shop story. This tale tips its hat to Creepy Magazine *and the classic horror comics from* EC Comics.

Pimm's Body Shop

Russ Crossley

THE SUN HAD SET BY THE TIME I STEPPED OUT OF THE DRIVING RAIN into the dingy, poorly lit shop on NW 2nd Avenue in Old Town. With trembling fingers cramped by cold, I reached into my jacket pocket for the card the warden had handed me before I left state prison to confirm this was the correct address. My eyes moved over the plain white card. Pimm's, Northwest second in navy blue lettering. This was the place, all right. I shoved the damp card back in my jacket pocket.

Released only two days ago, I was intent on my reintegration into society by seeking gainful employment. At least that's what it said in the pamphlet Warden Glen handed me during my release processing. He'd added, "See you soon, Bicks," with a sneer on his sweating, puffy features. I knew exactly what he meant. Ninety-nine percent of prisoners released from Oregon State Penitentiary in Salem were back behind bars within six months, and no one expected I would be in the one percent that made it on the outside.

Not that I blamed anyone for thinking I'd fail. After all, I had murdered a woman and her seventeen-year-old daughter in cold blood.

Pimm's Bodyshop

I used a knife—a bowie knife, to be exact—to gut them like fish. Why, you ask? Why not?

Fortunately, or depending on your point of view, unfortunately, the death penalty was off the table when I was convicted and sentenced to twenty-five years behind bars.

Now, twenty years later, I am a free man, paroled for good behavior, or, more likely, budget cuts. The fiscal reality these days is the state couldn't afford to house and feed me anymore on the very thin number of taxpayer dimes since the economy tanked in '08.

I almost burst out laughing when the warden told me I was a free man. Is he kidding? Free? Nope. Sorry, I'm a convicted murderer with no job history, no family, and no prospects. If I were a betting man, I'd have given myself five to one odds I'd die behind bars. But instead, dressed in my one good suit—the one they gave me when I was released—soaked through, trembling from the cold rainwater trickling down my neck, I stood in my cheap faux leather loafers on the scuffed wood floor of a tiny curio shop.

My arms hugged my lean frame tightly in a vain attempt to control my shivering. The air was stale as if no one had been in here in a very long time. It smelled of age, if that were a recognizable odor. There was a faint scent of mothballs, reminding me of the times my grandmother would fish out a shiny new penny from the piggy bank she kept on the top shelf of her closet.

Odd I should recall this particular memory after all the intervening years. The piggy bank was the first thing I ever stole. Very likely this theft set me on the path of lawlessness, resulting in the death of that woman and her daughter. I don't even remember their names anymore.

I still recall the girl's cheap, flowery, drugstore perfume and the thick coating of rouge on her high cheekbones that reminded me of my mother. The girl's mother let her dress like a whore. They had deserved to die.

My mother had been a whore who turned tricks when she wasn't stripping in the seedy bars where I spent my formative years. The prostitution paid for her drug habit, which eventually led to her contracting a disease later called AIDS. Of course this was a long time ago, but it seemed close to me in times of stress. Someone once said we are a product of our environment and I think my lack of respect for life supports that view.

Trying to get warm, I started walking amongst the shelves in the curio shop, studying the dust-coated curios interspersed among tattered books. The light inside the shop was minimal but I could still make out the titles on the spines. Next to a bleached human skull was a volume with the words *Encyclopedia of Black Magic* down the spine. The volume next to it read *The History of Zombification.* On the other side of the two thick books was a black onyx carving of a cat with yellow eyes that seemed to be watching me as I passed.

The next shelf was devoted to glass bottles labeled with the contents. There were the standard magic-spell items common to fairy tales such as eye of newt or bat wings; others were a little more unusual, such as toad heart and vampire blood.

A gruff, smoker's voice interrupted my investigation, startling me. "Can I help you?"

My heart pounding, I turned to find the shop owner you'd expect in such an establishment. Before me stood a hunched over old man of undeterminable age, with a fringe of white hair surrounding a wrinkled dome of gray flesh dotted with brown age spots.

Eyes as black as oil peered at me over reading glasses perched on a narrow nose, and the skin of his face and hands was leathery as if he'd spent too much time in the sun.

"Hello," I said. "No, I ducked into your shop to get out of the rain." I held up my arms and droplet of rain came off the sleeves, landing on the heavily marred wooden floor.

The corners of the old man's thin-lipped mouth curled up slightly while his eyes stayed flat and fixated on me. "Of course. Would you like a cup of tea?"

I dropped my arms to my sides. "Uh, yeah, sure, but do you have something stronger, perhaps?" The only alcohol I'd had in the past twenty years was the burning prison hooch aged two weeks at most. Some fine whiskey to ease the cold in my bones would be really welcome right now.

"Certainly. But you should be careful." He paused to lock eyes with me. "A man in your position can't be too careful. A drunkard gets a ticket back to the can sooner than you can spit."

I cocked an eyebrow. *How does he know I'm an ex-con?*

He turned away and began shuffling toward the rear of the shop. I immediately followed. Along the way I passed shelves brimming with more old books on such topics as the occult and a wide range of mythology from all over the world. Some tomes had titles related to the dark arts and magic, vampires, werewolves, and legendary monsters such as the Loch Ness monster and Bigfoot. Interspersed amongst the slowly rotting books were more curious objects. Some I recognized, while others were things I'd never seen before.

Miniature coffins, bottles that looked like black dirt, and a bottle that reminded me of an old mayonnaise jar filled with eyeballs floating in a slightly cloudy liquid. My stomach twitched at the sight of the disembodied eyes.

I had been studying to become a doctor before I succumbed to the urge to murder the girl and her mother. Body parts didn't bother me, but the thought of saving them in a rinsed-out mayo jar sure did. I may be a killer, but I'm not a monster.

Finally the old man led me into a dingy office. Against one wall was a shaded desk lamp resting on a well-worn pine desk peppered with stacks of paper. There was no computer, and between the desk and the wall was an army-green, four-drawer, metal filing cabinet. A yellowing map of the world was attached to the wall above the desk, held in place by plastic-tipped cherry-red pushpins on the four corners. Otherwise the whitewashed walls were bare.

The room appeared to be no more than five feet by five feet in size, but when I entered, the room seemed much larger. It occurred to me I had entered the *Twilight Zone* except I didn't see Rod Serling. There were even two captain's chairs. The old man eased into the one behind the desk as he waved me into the other. The creak of the dry wood echoed off the walls when I eased myself down. I ran my tongue over my dry lips and my heart pounded against my ribs. The walls felt like they were closing in, as if I were in prison again.

The corners of the old man's mouth curled again, but this time his eyes smiled. My eyes shifted to a dusky, legal-size file folder on the desk in front of him between the stacks of papers.

"Curious?"

I nodded.

He slid the middle drawer of the filing cabinet open and took out a half full bottle and two relatively clean glasses. After unscrewing the cap, he poured two fingers of whiskey in each glass, then put the bottle away. He handed me a glass, the smoky whiskey swirling. The earthy scent hit my nostrils and I shivered with delight. I took a sip.

Pimm's Bodyshop

The burning liquid slid easily past my lips, over my tongue, and down my throat. I'd never tasted anything so heavenly.

He grunted a chuckle. "I know you're wondering how I know you who you are, Mr. Bicks, since we've never met." He patted the folder on his desk with one gnarled hand. Under the soft glow of the desk lamp, his skin appeared almost translucent. "In this folder is everything about you, including the details of your family and your prison record."

My stomach knotted and the long-buried anger of my youth surged from back of my throat. "Who are you?" I couldn't keep the menace from my voice. In my head I had already begun planning the disposal of his corpse if it turned out he knew too much about me. If this old man told potential employers about my background, my chances of making it on the outside were greatly reduced, and I planned to prove the warden wrong. No one, not even this old man, would stand in my way.

In response the old man chuckled, evidently unafraid of what I might do to him. I set the glass on the desk next to his. "Don't worry, Mr. Bicks, I'm not your enemy. My name's Pimm, Skip Pimm, and the fact is, I want to hire you for a job." His eyes narrowed. "A very special job."

My anger subsided but my instinct for self-preservation was still on full alert. "Is it legal? I can't go back to prison." And I meant it. Twenty years was long enough. I'd done my duty to the state so I was damned if I was going back to the joint.

The old man nodded. "Don't worry, Mr. Bicks, there is no way they will be able to send you back to prison." He lowered his voice as if someone would overhear us. "They can't arrest you if they don't know it's you."

"Plastic surgery?"

Russ Crossley

"No, nothing so crude."

"All right, old man, what's the catch? If it's not plastic surgery, then what? A mask, like in those *Mission Impossible* movies?"

The old man smiled and stood up. His back was really bent; he stooped so far over I thought he'd fall on his face. He smelled of formaldehyde. "Follow me. What I'm going to show you will either leave you begging for the job or we'll part company and you'll never hear from me again."

"Why should I trust you?"

"Because I know you'll take the job. It will change your life."

Now he really had my attention. My life so far had been on the fast road to hell, a change of any kind had to be better than where I was headed.

Pimm exited the office ahead of me, shuffling as he walked to the rear of the shop. I was surprised when the old man stopped by a large section of blank wall. I'd assumed all the walls had storage shelves filled with macabre items. In fact, next to the empty wall was a shelving unit filled with shrunken heads. Pimm placed a hand flat on a section of wall to his right. After an audible click, a section of blank wall swung away from us. Pimm felt around in the inky darkness inside until, with another click, a light came on illuminating a staircase that disappeared into more darkness below.

"What's this?"

Pimm glanced at me. "My laboratory. Actually, I call it Pimm's body shop."

Laboratory? Had I somehow stepped into Frankenstein's castle? I eyed Pimm. Is this old man Igor? The hunch in his back certainly supported my hypothesis.

"Shall we?" he asked before starting down the stairs ahead of me.

Pimm's Bodyshop

For one of the few times in my life, I experienced fear. My heart was beating fast, my mouth was dry, and my legs trembled. I licked my lips, then made my decision.

***

When I arrived at the bottom of the stairs, Pimm flicked another switch. The light revealed a large storeroom with steel shelving units containing cardboard boxes lining three of the walls. At the opposite end of the room was a steel door with a numbered keypad instead of a key lock. I had half expected to find an old-fashioned dungeon door, the kind that was unlocked with a massive brass key. But this room, unlike the shop above, was neatly organized and spotless, so it clearly wasn't a classical interpretation of a dungeon.

"What's behind the door?" I asked.

Without responding, Pimm walked to the door and keyed in a sequence of four numbers, then pulled the handle. The door swung into the storage room. The room was a vast cave, and against the far wall were two chambers resting on stands that reminded me of coffins except they had glass, half-moon-shaped domes instead of lids. Each one appeared to be large enough to hold a human.

I entered the cavern and moved to stand over the chambers. The glass covers allowed me see what they contained. My breath caught in my throat. Inside were two bodies, one male, one female, both very human, or at least humanoid. Ten fingers, ten toes is the usual test, and they were physically perfect specimens. Since they were naked, my ability to identify the sex and species was relatively easy, but the question now was, were they real?

"Ummm, Mr. Pimm, I think it's time for you to explain what this is all about."

***

Sitting again in the chair in his tiny office, I listened intently to the old man's story. Pimm had given me a couple of tattered towels so I could dry off. I had dried my hair and doffed my suit jacket, which now hung over the back of the chair. The rain had penetrated through to my skin, and my clothes were still saturated by the frigid water. I had the second towel draped over my shoulders hugging my neck. I nipped at the whiskey he'd given me earlier, careful not to drink too much no matter how good it tasted or how much it warmed my insides. I needed a clear head if the fantastic tale he'd been weaving for the past hour was true.

In addition to owning this curio shop, Pimm was an inventor. He had designed and built the twin stasis chambers—as he called them—over thirty years ago for him and his wife. If either of them contracted an incurable disease, their body would be preserved until a cure could be found in the future. Unfortunately, his wife died before she could be preserved. Despondent over the loss of his one true love, Pimm abandoned the idea and stored the stasis chambers in the cave.

Years later a mysterious man came into his shop claiming to be a time traveler. He was desperate and said he was dying. The man offered Pimm what he called a time receptor, a device that acted as a beacon at one end of a controlled wormhole between two points in time. Before Pimm could determine the truth and ask where in time the man claimed to be from, the man died. Pimm dumped the body in a landfill and dismissed his wild claims as the ramblings of a sick man.

Thinking nothing more about the device—he said it was shaped like a small pyramid, one sold to tourists—or it's alleged origin, he buried the thing at the back of a shelf in his shop and forgot about it until a year ago when a young couple appeared saying they, too, were time travelers. They told him they desperately needed the device to transport themselves to their own time. In the future, common diseases like measles, mumps, and even the common cold virus have been eradicated. The time travelers' immune systems were unable to cope with twenty-first-century infections. The air itself was killing them.

Though Pimm searched every shelf in the shop, he was unable to find the device again before the two time travelers slipped into comas. Deciding he had little choice, he sealed their unconscious bodies in the stasis chambers. Their vital signs stabilized but they remained comatose.

I cleared my throat after taking another small sip of the burning whiskey; the smoky smell of the liquor still filled my nostrils. "So why are you telling me all this?"

Pimm eyed me with one bushy gray eyebrow cocked. "I had a plan for me and my wife." He lowered his tone. "A dangerous plan. Very risky."

Now he had me intrigued. I set the glass on the desk and leaned closer to him, locking eyes with the old man. "Dangerous, huh? Like what?"

"I invented a memory engram transfer encoder. I can swap memories between brains."

I eased back in the chair, causing it to creak in the tiny office. I knew what he was planning. Before Mrs. Pimm died, he must have planned to transfer their memories into new bodies to extend their lives.

But they would need bodies—the brains, to be exact—of two subjects younger than themselves. No one would volunteer for such a procedure and unhealthy subjects wouldn't do, but two young, beautiful bodies had conveniently dropped into his lap, or rather entered his shop.

"But I thought you said the two time travelers' immune systems had been compromised?"

He nodded. "I gave them blood transfusions so their systems would be recalibrated for our time period. According to the tests, their bodies are healthy and able to survive in our time frame. I've kept them sedated waiting for your arrival."

"Why me?" This was the million-dollar question.

The corners of Pimm's mouth curled upward and he dropped his hands into his lap, interlocking his fingers. "You are an ex-con with no prospects, no family, and no job; and you have medical training, which could come in handy. In other words, Mr. Bicks, you are perfect for what I have in mind."

I then realized why I had been released early. "Warden Glen set this up, didn't he?"

Pimm nodded. "I paid him to find the perfect man for my experiment, a man with nothing to lose and everything to gain from a new body. Is a fresh start in life worth something to you?"

I eyed the hunchbacked old man. He was mad. But I decided to play along, for now. "OK, Mr. Pimm, what's next?"

I don't know why, but his snag-toothed smile made me shiver.

***

Pimm's Bodyshop

Over the next few days, I helped Pimm prepare the bodies and set up a device that looked like a portable drill similar to the ones dentists used, only much larger. At the end of one flexible arm was a cone-shaped outlet that he said would be placed over the top of the subject's skull. An identical arm was attached to the other side of the stand from which both arms sprang. The base of the stand was barrel shaped and contained circuit boards and a large capacity microprocessor that Pimm explained held upwards of five hundred million yottabytes of information. This was the most powerful processor ever built. This device was designed to transfer brain engrams between the subjects.

I bought the most powerful, heavy-duty portable generator on the market and tied it into the power source for the stasis chambers. The transfer would draw a lot of power from the city power grid, and if the grid overloaded, it might shut down. If that happened, then our new homes might die before the transfer was complete.

Pimm wanted me to inhabit the female body, but I planned to murder him before the transfer, then transfer my memory engrams into the male body. I had watched him setting up and calibrating the memory transfer device and studied his research extensively. By now I figured I knew more about the memory engram transfer encoder than he did.

Finally the day arrived. We would complete the transfer at three a.m. when the power grid was at its lowest utilization, and staffing at the city power plant was at minimum levels so they wouldn't be able to dedicate staff to trace the drain back to us too quickly. We planned to be done long before they discovered the source of the drain.

I had acquired another bowie knife, which I had strapped to my belt hidden beneath the calf-length lab coat Pimm had provided me.

At two thirty we were sitting in his office, each with a shot of whisky in a glass, toasting to our impending success. The burning liquor slid easily down my throat and I smiled at Pimm, who looked happy to witness the fruit of a lifetime of labors. His eyes drooped at the corners when he set the empty glass on the desk.

"Something wrong?" I asked.

He looked at me. "I was thinking about my wife, Ana. She would have been proud of me. Too bad she can't be here."

I chuckled. "Wherever she is, I'm certain she's proud of you."

"I suppose. But if only she hadn't died." He looked away and slid a desk draw open behind him. His body blocked my view but his arm moved as he took something out of the drawer.

It was a folded picture frame, the kind that held two photographs. He set it on the desk between us. "Take a look," he said.

I opened the picture frame to reveal a picture of a middle-aged woman with brown hair streaked with threads of gray. The other picture was of a teenage girl. "Who are they?" I asked.

He sighed. "My wife and daughter. They were murdered."

I opened my mouth to speak, but a sudden wave of dizziness swept over me. My eyes felt heavy and my pulse was rapid. My mouth was suddenly dry as sandpaper. "I don't feel so good."

"You killed my family." Pimm's words drifted off, and as if someone had turned out a light, darkness enveloped me.

***

I don't know how long I was unconscious, but when I awoke, I was looking at the slightly distorted black lava rock of the cave's ceiling. I realized I was alive but my body felt strange.

73

Pimm's Bodyshop

I can only describe the sensation as being out of balance as if my arms, legs, and torso had changed in size and dimensions.

Had Pimm completed the experiment? Was I in my new body? I tilted my head forward as much as possible, given the glass cover was only inches from my face. Female breasts? He'd transferred my memories into the woman's body after all. I dropped my head back and closed my eyes. Damn him. He'd drugged me. Pimm must have suspected I'd pull something. The old man was smart, but I'd still kill him.

As my eyes fluttered open, I found myself looking into the face of the old man hovering over the stasis chamber's glass cover. "I see you're awake," he said, his voice slightly muffled by the glass as if I were underwater. "Good. I have a surprise for you." He chuckled. Not the friendly Santa Claus kind of chuckle, more the Darth Vader kind.

My heart rate increased and my fear of enclosed spaces twisted in my guts. Panic was building in me. "Mr. Pimm, please let me out." Why wasn't he in his new body?

I heard the hiss of air and a slight breeze brushed against my bare feet. What was he doing, gassing me? I detected the scent of damp air of the cave; the sharp scent of the lava rock was very distinct. He'd opened the vents in the foot of the chamber to the outside air. Why?

Pimm's round face reappeared, his dark eyes sparking with glee. "You murdered my wife and daughter twenty years ago. Mr. Bicks. Now you'll finally pay for your crime."

What was he talking about? The woman and the girl in those picture frames on his desk came back to me. I knew them. Memories flooded my mind of those women's terrified faces, pleading for their lives before I silenced them by slitting their throats.

74

I killed his wife and daughter.

"Listen, Pimm, I'm sorry, I had no idea who they were." I struggled to lift my arms from my sides but the curve of the chamber walls prevented me from raising them. "Please let me out!" My eyes filled with tears. "Please! I hate enclosed spaces."

Pimm emitted a grim chuckle. "Don't worry, your suffering will be over soon. But not too soon." His eyes drooped slightly. "I thought about slashing you open with your bowie knife as you did my wife and daughter, but that would be too easy a death." His eyes narrowed. "I want you to suffer before you die. An agonizing death is justice for your crimes. You are going to suffocate from within."

"What do you mean?"

Pimm shrugged. "I lied. The blood transfusion on the two bodies in the stasis chambers didn't work. The body you now inhabit is dying.

The stasis chambers kept them alive while I waited for you to be released. It took me years to save enough money to bribe the warden.

"I estimate the pneumonia in the woman's body will soon do the job quite nicely that the state was unwilling to do.

Within a day your lungs will fill with liquid and you'll drown in your own body fluids. You ever try holding your breath for an extended period?"

No. It couldn't be. My new body shivered and beads of sweat broke out all over my flesh. My face felt hot and I shivered. "I'm sorry, Pimm, I'm sorry. That must count for something?"

He shook his head. "No, Bicks, it doesn't. I hope you appreciate the irony of dying in a woman's body. I know I do." He disappeared from my view and the laboratory dropped into darkness. '

Pimm's Bodyshop

The last sounds I heard were the steel door sliding shut across the cave floor, then the thump of it settling into place and the click as the lock was engaged.

My fate was sealed in this new body. I began to sob.

Life is all about change, growing older, having children, getting married, falling in love. Change is a constant that many people fear. This story demonstrates change is sometimes welcome and inevitable.

Moon Spell

Rita Schulz

LUCY, A PRETTY, SLENDER GIRL IN HER LATE TEENS, stood in the middle of the large, bright, country kitchen leaning on her broom, worrying about Tom, her brother. She hadn't seen him in a very long time, and then it had been only a very short visit.

They lived in the little village of Squamish, which lies in the shadow of the Pacific Coast Range, just outside Vancouver, British Columbia. A very small town that lots of people passed by on the Sea to Sky Highway on their way to the resort town of Whistler, but few ever stopped.

"Lucy, you can't do anything about it, so you may as well stop fretting. It happened a long time ago. You know that the odds of turning that boy back into a human after all this time are little to none."

Lucy looked at Nona, a tall, grey-haired woman, the town's friendly wise woman, and smiled at her. Lucy went back to sweeping the old wooden farmhouse floor as she had promised to do, but her mind was firmly set on this problem that her brother had accidentally created, and affected her directly.

Their family was cursed to wander the earth. They would never be able to settle anywhere for any length of time.

Tom had accidently turned his best friend Cory into a werewolf, and Cory had in turn cursed the family. Now the only way to fix everything was to cure Cory. Simple. At least Lucy thought so.

"I know that, but is there anything else that can be done? It's not like Tom meant to hurt his friend and turn him into a werewolf. He actually did his friend a favor. It was a case of him dying or drinking the potion. And he chose…"

"Stop it, Lucy! That's enough. The University judged him, found him guilty, and now his fate is sealed. He'll wander all his life and never find rest," said Nona. Her voice was sad, but firm, as she peeled a batch of potatoes for dinner.

Nona was as frustrated as Lucy, but she couldn't let the young girl know that.

What Nona didn't say was that Lucy would have the same fate to wander as her brother when she got older, since the curse was on Tom and his family. Their parents were dead and it hadn't affected Nona, at least not yet.

Nona wasn't sure when Lucy would start to wander, and kept a sharp eye on her. She had tried to prepare the girl as best she could.

"I know, but I do miss him."

"Me, too. I can't help but think that he would have made a great wizard, but something really went wrong."

Nona went out into the backyard to work in her garden, leaving Lucy to finish her chores.

There was a ring of the doorbell. Lucy went to open the front door. She was surprised to see the UPS man in his brown uniform, with a package tucked under his arm.

"Mrs. Thompson?" he asked. He smiled at Lucy with a slightly wolfish grin. His large brown eyes scanned around the room. Finally his eyes settled on Lucy.

Lucy looked up at the tall, dark-haired man and smiled at him, too.

He certainly wasn't hard on the eyes, being your typically tall, dark, and handsome male type.

"I'll call Nona for you," said Lucy.

"No worries. Tell you what, I'll just leave the package for your grandmother—it's her little book, *Kitchen Magic*—and take you with me," said the man as he dropped the old, faded, dark blue book on the coffee table and swept Lucy up into his arms. One hand covered her mouth and the other held her firmly around the waist.

Lucy heard Nona call to her as she was swept out the door. She tried to yell, but she couldn't with the man's hand so tightly held against her mouth.

She struggled, trying to kick him, then she tried to use her elbows, but he was too strong and held her tight.

Fear rose in her belly and her heart beat hard against her chest. He carried her out of the door, down the path to his idling truck. The only thing to do was to bite him hard, as hard as she could, so he would drop her.

She drew back her lips and opened her mouth as wide as she could. She knew that she would only get one chance at this.

"Don't try it, Lucy. I'm Cory. The man your brother turned into a werewolf. If you bite me, we don't know what my blood will do to you. It could turn you into a werewolf, too. Don't forget I was turned by magic."

She was shocked and stopped fighting. His voice was low and guttural, almost like a vicious dog's snarl as he spoke.

He quickly tied her up, gagged her, and threw her into the back of the truck.

Lucy tried to think of some way of escaping and not of what would happen next to her, but her mind went there anyway.

She pulled against her bonds, trying to get her hands and feet loose, but nothing would give. She was tied too well. She focused on trying to loosen the ropes; she wouldn't give up.

Was he going to kill her? But if that was what he wanted, he could have done that already. She thought of different possible solutions, finally realizing that all she could do was wait and see. She knew that she would find a way out of this situation—she had too.

It was a long drive, but the twists and turns were familiar to her. Soon they were out past Whistler, then they turned onto a little-used gravel back road that even Lucy wasn't familiar with. It seemed to her that her body was being shaken apart with all the ruts and potholes the truck hit.

She fell asleep.

She found herself waking up when the shaking and the crunch of gravel under the tires stopped.

She woke confused and disorientated. She tried to stretch her legs, but when she couldn't move, she remembered where she was and that she was tied up. Fear bubbled to the surface inside of her.

It was late afternoon, almost dusk. She knew that night would be falling soon since it was getting dark in the truck.

She wondered if Cory would turn into a wolf tonight.

The back of the truck opened and there he stood. She waited until he got closer and tried to kick him with her bound legs. He just stepped to one side and smiled at her.

She was afraid of him.

She reminded herself he was a killer. That's what werewolves were. Natural killers.

He picked her up as if she weighed nothing, put her over his shoulder, and carried her inside a small cottage. The drapes were drawn and it was dark. He carried her into the living room and dropped her onto the couch. It was a rough old red thing that scratched her cheek and smelled like wet dog.

Lucy let out a small exclamation as the air rushed out of her lungs.

How dare he drop me like an old sack of potatoes?

She heard him rattle around in the kitchen and smelt wood smoke. Then his heavy footsteps came back into the living room.

"Lucy, listen to me," he said and turned his back to her.

She felt something cold and hard touch her ankle and then she heard a soft click. She tensed at the sound. What had he done to her?

She craned her head to see what was happening, but couldn't see anything because his body blocked her view.

His strong hands grabbed her under her armpits and pulled her into a sitting position. She saw that she now had a metal ring around her ankle, attached to a long chain that was anchored to the floor.

Lucy's mouth went dry with fear and she realized he was planning to keep her captive for a long time.

"Lucy, I'm going to untie you now, but as you see, you can't get away. And there aren't any neighbors for about five miles, so no one will hear you scream. All you're going to do is hurt yourself if you try."

As Cory said this, he untied her ankles and wrists and finally he removed the duct tape from her mouth. It ripped her skin and her eyes teared up, but she refused to let it show. She was determined to maintain her outward control.

"What do you want with me? You've already cursed my family. What more do you want?"

"It's getting late so we'll have to talk about that tomorrow. Right now you need to know a few things. The chain you have around you ankle is very strong and very long. There is a small shed at the back of the cottage and I need you to lock me into it. This is for your own safety. You will let me out in the morning because I have the keys to the truck and the supplies, which are out of your reach. Without food and water, you will die."

"Why are you doing this?"

She watched him closely and one of her questions was being answered. She saw his eyes start to grow larger, rounder, and a deeper brown.

"Quickly, this is your one key for the shed. Follow me," he said as he handed her a new brass key.

Lucy got up, fighting the pins and needles in her legs and arms, and followed him as quickly as she could.

There was a small, new outbuilding behind the cottage and out of sight from the road. It looked sturdy and was made of heavy timbers. It only had one door in the front. There was a small barred window beside the door.

"I need you to lock me into the Kennel. Quickly now, it's getting dark."

Cory opened the door, turned, and closed it.

Lucy stood at the door. The chain on her ankle was tight but it had reached its end.

She smiled at Cory and locked him into the building, then stepped back.

She now had all the power.

Twilight had come and the sky had turned a dark orange, then a deep purple as the stars appeared in the clear sky.

"Sleep well, Lucy," said the werewolf as the last part of his humanness faded. He became a wolf.

There was another, larger outbuilding on the other side of the house, one she couldn't reach, just like the truck that was parked too far for her to get to.

Lucy went back into the house and smelled hot stew. Her stomach growled. She realized that he had heated the stew for her supper. The smell made her mouth water and she realized how hungry she was.

The cottage had two large bedrooms. One was empty and the second had a large bed in it.

Lucy was petrified. She had to find a way out of this place before morning. She got up and headed for the wood box that she had seen at the back of the cottage next to the kitchen door; she hoped that she would find an axe. It was empty except for a good supply of chopped wood.

Next she searched through all the cupboards and drawers in the kitchen. She looked for anything that she could use as a tool to help her get the iron ring out of the floor or the metal bracelet off her ankle. All that she found were some pots, pans, and spoons.

She made a quick but thorough check of the closets and any other area that may hide any tools. Nothing.

She started to shiver and realized that the cabin was getting cold now that the sun had disappeared and went to start a fire in the fireplace. There was a fire all laid out and ready for her. Soon she has a nice warm fire. She picked up the wood poker to move the logs over and her heart jumped as she looked at the poker. This might be her answer.

Moon Spell

She quickly went over to the ring in the floor and realized that the handle was too wide to fit the ring and the other end of the poker was too wide, too. Neither end would fit into the ring.

Lucy realized that if she used the bottom of the poker, she might be able to use it as a pivot point to pull up and loosen the ring. It worked. She still has a very long length of chain attached to her ankle, but she was free.

Lucy knew that she was miles away from anyone, but if she stayed on the roads, she was confident that she would come across someone.

The moon was bright and it helped as she walked down the gravel road. Around her owls hooted on the hunt and the trees rustled in the cool breeze.

Then she heard a heavy, pacing sound in the bushes and quickened her pace. Lucy heard it again and stopped. The sound stopped as well.

Lucy started walking again and felt a set of eyes on her. She heard the yowl of a large cat. Was she being hunted? She heard it again. The sound seemed closer. She finally panicked and broke into a run.

She looked behind her. There in the moonlight was a large cougar. It lifted its muzzle into the air and started toward Lucy again. It was getting closer.

Then she heard the snarl of a wolf close by. The sound terrified her, but for some reason also made her feel hopeful.

She left the road and took cover behind a wide old evergreen next to a large clump of rocks.

She watched the wolf attack the cougar. Lucy rooted for the wolf. She hoped he didn't get hurt. The cat attacked quickly and tried to claw the wolf's belly.

84

The wolf twisted just in time to avoid the lethal strike and turned to grab the cat's neck from behind and shook it hard.

The wolf was much larger and heavier than the cat, and the cat realized it. The cat made another attempt, but gave up what it thought was an easy meal, turned, and ran into the woods.

At first Lucy was happy the wolf won, but soon her feelings turn cold as the wolf turned and walked slowly toward her. He snarled, his razor-like fangs showing clearly, his head hung low, his yellow eyes studying her.

Was this Cory, the werewolf, or was this a wild wolf on the hunt for a meal?

She looked around for something to defend herself with and only found a handful of small, loose rocks. She gathered them up.

The wolf approached her. Fear coursed through her body making her hands wet with perspiration.

Am I going to die now?

She forced herself to keep breathing, to keep staring down the wolf, to face her fear. She gripped the rocks tightly, ready to throw them.

As the wolf grew closer, it stopped and changed into a man.

Her fear ebbed and she realized she was holding the rocks so tightly that they were cutting into her palms. Since it hurt, she dropped the sharp stones and came out from her hiding place.

"You lied to me," said Lucy as she wiped her wet, gritty hands on her jeans. "There was another way out of the Kennel."

"Good thing for you there was. Come on," he said and started to walk with an easy stride back to the cottage. He seemed casual and confident in his own skin.

"You can change your shape when you want to? You're not governed by the moon?"

He shrugged his shoulders but didn't answer.

The gravel road was rough and she had to make sure that she didn't step in any large potholes.

"My brother made a mistake. There must be something you can do to reverse the potion's effects," said Lucy, her voice soft in the night air.

Cory snorted, a soft sound, and shook his head. "Do you think I'm stupid and haven't tried? I've gone to the University, to my own doctor, and to anyone else that I could think of. No one could help me."

Lucy sighed; she felt stupid and bad for Cory. But she held on to her belief that someone could help him.

"What was my brother using when he tried to cure you?"

"What do you mean?"

"What spell or potions book was he using? Something from you classes?"

They finally got to the cottage and went in. Lucy hadn't realized how cold it was outside and started to shiver. She wasn't sure if it was from the cold outside or if it was a delayed reaction to everything that she had gone through that day.

She sat down on the couch. "Well? Was it one of the books from your courses or from somewhere else?"

"It was an old, faded, dark blue book that he ran and got," he said as he went into the second bedroom. He came out a few minutes later, barefoot and wearing a pair of old blue jeans and a black tee shirt.

"I know what we need to do," said Lucy as she watched Cory lean down and throw another log onto the fire.

She watched him and waited until he looked at her. She knew that she would need his undivided attention.

"What, you know of a good witch doctor for me to see?"

"No, you need to see Nona and Tom," she said.

She suddenly realized that she really wanted to help Cory. He had cursed her family, but she still wanted to help him.

"It sounds like it was Nona's old spell book *Kitchen Magic* that Tom was using, and if he made a mistake, then maybe they can work on figuring it out."

"I'm not going to repeat myself. Nothing is going to help me."

"Look, before you get all defensive, it's worth a try," she said as quickly as she could.

Lucy looked him right in the eyes, waiting for him to react and get angry.

She had never been more afraid in her life, not for herself, but that he would refuse to get help.

Cory's shoulders dropped and she knew that she had won, at least this first round.

"Why did you bring me here?"

"Why not? I'm tired of living in isolation."

"Is that why you brought me here? Because you're afraid of hurting someone as a wolf?"

He didn't answer her, but came over and unlocked the ring around her ankle.

He quietly turned and went out the back door, turned into a wolf, and ran into the dark woods.

Lucy closed the door behind him.

She sat on the couch, exhausted, but her mind wouldn't rest as it went over everything that had happened to her today. As well as everything she had remembered about the story, the mistake her brother had made, and the curse on the family.

She was sure that if she could get everyone to Nona's, they would be able to fix this.

***

The morning dawned bright and the blue jays in the evergreens woke her.

She sat up and realized that she had fallen asleep on the couch and had a bad crick in her neck.

She could hear someone in the kitchen and the smell and sizzle of bacon. She felt her stomach rumbled with hunger pangs. The smell of freshly brewed coffee filled the cottage and she smiled to herself. She could get used to someone making her breakfast in the mornings.

She went into the kitchen and sat down on one of the old oak chairs behind the large wooden table.

She felt good and positive this morning. She knew that she was on the right track in getting Cory fixed and the curse off their family.

Cory put a platter of bacon, eggs, and toast on the table and sat down next to her. They quickly filled their plates and both started to eat.

"Lucy, I'm going to take you back home this morning," said Cory as he bit off and chewed a piece of toast.

Lucy nodded silently as she took a bite of her eggs and waited for him to continue.

She waited, but he didn't say anything more. She felt confused, but thought that it was wisest not to say anything right now. This wasn't the right time or place.

They left right after breakfast. The ride was long, but quiet. It seemed that both of them were deep in their own thoughts.

They finally arrived in front of Nona's home and she got out. She turned to wait for Cory, but he stayed in the truck.

She went around to his side of the truck and he rolled down his window. She looked into his deep, warm brown eyes and smiled.

"I'm not coming in with you. I've taken the curse off. You and your family are free from it."

"Why? Why don't you want to come in? I'm sure that Nona could help you," said Lucy.

She heard desperation creep into her voice and stopped herself. Lucy knew that she should be happy that the curse was off her family, and she was, but it wasn't enough. She also wanted to help Cory.

The front door of the house opened, and before she knew it, Tom and Nona both hugged her.

Tom looked at Cory.

"I'm sorry," said Tom.

Cory nodded.

"Come into the house please, Cory," said Nona.

Cory sat, looking at them and shaking his head.

"I've taken the curse off your family."

"We know. Thank you. Now please come in. I think we have something for you as well."

"Actually, I have been thinking about it and I've decided to stay the way I am, at least for right now. Can I get a rain check if I decide to change my mind?" asked Cory, smiling.

Lucy was confused. She thought he would want to be human again.

But he hadn't attacked her last night, so maybe he didn't need to live in isolation any longer.

Perhaps he finally realized that he wouldn't hurt anyone after all, and it was only his fear of himself that kept him in isolation.

Then she realized he was human and could take on the wolf form whenever he wanted to.

Maybe now he did have the best of both worlds.

One of the great unknowns is the eternal question of life after death. Theologians and philosophers alike have debated this question for centuries. Are ghosts and spirits real? What happens after our mortal body dies? This unusual tale tells the very personal story of a man who discovers that the answers to these questions are too close to home.

The Eliminators

Russ Crossley

"IMPOSSIBLE..." I BREATHED.

The rapid beating of my heart eclipsed the incessant growl of big-city traffic coming from the street below the office window.

It—the spectral figure—levitated a meter above the scored and heavily traveled hardwood floor of our cramped, dusty office.

We're located in a two-story walk-up near the corner of Main and Hastings Streets on the east side of Vancouver. Harry and I have operated our PI business from the 50-plus-year-old office building for the past five years. I sometimes forget five years has passed since we opened The Eliminators Paranormal Investigative Service together as partners. Most people called us The Eliminators for short. (I certainly prefer this over the unflattering E-PIS our detractors call us.)

The Eliminators

The truth is, we are secretly under contract to the City of Vancouver's finest. Not that the VPD chief would ever admit we often work for the cops when they are faced with unexplained paranormal crime. The chief's office is just two blocks from where I stand, yet he has never even set foot inside our door.

His kiss-ass assistant, Blake "Blakey" Thomas, acts as his intermediary. Blakey is such a weasel.

The press dubs us the Ghostbusters, named, I suppose, after that Dan Aykroyd movie in the eighties. In reality, we had never seen an actual ghost until this moment. And the one standing before me looked very much like my mother.

I shivered in the cold air. Unusual for an August afternoon when the outside temperature neared forty degrees Celsius, and normally even warmer in here.

The woman-shaped phantom stood, or should I say floated, on the opposite side of my scarred, forties-era pine desk, and indeed looked the spitting image of my mother. Except for the dark, pupil-less eyes, she could easily pass as Mom's doppelganger. A twin, maybe. A dead twin, perhaps, but still a mirror image of my mother.

Not that I knew if dear old Mom was alive or dead. I hadn't seen her in a *long* time.

Dressed in tan walking shorts, a mustard-yellow sleeveless tee shirt, and brown leather sandals, Mom's ensemble must be all the rage amongst the best-dressed ghosts these days. Her gaze was unflinchingly fixed on me.

"Uh…what…what…do you want…" I managed to stammer from between frozen lips. The sweetened coffee I had been sipping turned sour in my mouth.

Out of the corner of one eye, I saw my partner Harry his tree-trunk-like legs were crossed atop his equally ancient desk.

His muscular fingers were laced across his wide chest and his cool blue eyes were fixated on the ghost. That was Harry. Cool as the proverbial cucumber.

He had been in the process of writing up the invoice for our latest client when the ghost suddenly appeared.

Mr. Wallace had hired us to follow his wife, who he thought was unfaithful.

For this one we didn't even have to leave the office. Easy money. Harry's gift for foretelling the future meant he had seen Mrs. Wallace's lover's death in a seven-car pile-up on Route One. It was going to rain hard the next day and Harry saw the guy's green Dodge Ram roll over and burst into flames. The guy was barbecue.

An ugly scene, true, but it meant some much-needed funds would join their meager cousins in our bank account.

Poor Harry. He didn't much care for his so-called "gift" in cases like the guy with the truck. I had to agree, seeing and feeling the guy's terror as he burned to death was not much of a gift.

Though he is able to see future events, Harry is unable to change them in any way. If he saw the country was about to be nuked, he would be helpless to stop it. Sure, he could warn people and leave the country himself, but the nukes would still fall. Talk about the ultimate raw deal.

Me? I can move stuff with my mind. I always figured that was why Mom left us and Dad drank himself to death. They just couldn't handle my gift.

In the Wallaces' case, Mrs. Wallace would not be cheating with that guy again. And she wouldn't cheat with anyone else. Harry had seen that, as well.

I offered my opinion that Mrs. Wallace must have really loved the guy—the lover, not the husband.

Harry wasn't so sure. He thought Mrs. Wallace was damned scared of what might happen to her, that she suspected her husband was behind the accident. Kinda like that Harrison Ford movie about a lawyer whose wife murders his mistress. Being in the PI business means you encounter a lot of loonies.

For five years we have been at this location, and for five years we have been trying, without success, to move The Eliminators Paranormal Investigative Service up the PI food chain. We are eager to get closer to the really big bucks downtown. Simple, really. If only we could snag one of those upscale clients—and if the press would stop calling us a couple of nuts—then we might stand a real chance at success.

The slumlord that runs this two-story walk-up demands more rent every year. This means we have less and less for the luxuries, like food.

"You can't be my mother," I said to the silent apparition. "I haven't seen her in fifteen years. Nor do I want to again. Ever."

To emphasize my point, I used my telekinesis to fly a white china coffee cup off the makeshift shelf I had installed over the drip coffee pot directly at her head. It passed through her, then shattered with a loud bang against the opposite wall, near the sagging gray metal file cabinet.

Harry sighed. "Do ya really have to do that?"

"Sorry. I—"

"You have to kill me," said the ghost suddenly. Her voice was soft and echoed as if she were speaking from inside a steel drum.

Harry suddenly fell backward to land with a loud bang against the cheap tile floor. "Oh. My. God," he said.

A shiver ran through me. Harry knew something. His gift was telling him something—something bad.

His face was pale, as pale as the white dress shirt he wore under his smoke-gray suit jacket. I hated his ties, but never said so—to his face, anyway. This one was a ghastly floral pattern.

Do something, numb nuts, I said to myself. But it was as if I were frozen where I stood. Fear gripped me and my limbs refused to respond to my brain's instructions.

I detected a faint odor of ozone in the air. It was as if an electrical charge surrounded the ghost of my mother. *This is too weird.*

"My son, you were always useless," she said.

I didn't have to listen to this crap. Before I could stop myself, years of pent-up frustration and anger spilled out of me. "You ran out on us. Dad was devastated—I was only twelve."

"All true. But that's not the whole truth." The ghost of Mary Alice O'Shay turned to face me. "Your father beat me. Or had your forgotten about that part of our happy home life?"

I felt my ears grow warm. "No. But Dad had—issues."

"Dad was a drunk." She snorted in disgust.

Now as I said, Harry and I had never seen a real ghost before. We had certainly uncovered a few frauds, but this spirit didn't look like faked special effects. Not like the case Harry and I solved when the disgraced special effects guy used SFX to scare a widow out of her family fortune.

He'd blackmailed her by haunting her with her deceased husband's ghost. The "ghost" said she had murdered him for his money. All true, of course, she had certainly murdered her husband ten years before. But the special effects guy just could not resist the urge to use his talents to fool the old lady. Scared her to death. Heart attack.

We caught the special effects guy the old-fashioned way. Too bad, really. At the time,

I thought it would be nice to see the ghost of her dead husband. Now I wasn't so certain.

"Uh, Jimmy…" said Harry. "I don't wanta interrupt your family reunion, but it seems to me we have a larger issue here. Like why is a ghost standing in our office?"

Mary chuckled. "Of course. Harry's right. James, you and I will have to work through this baggage of ours later. Besides, there isn't a lot of time."

"For what?" I asked. My eyes narrowed while my voice echoed my suspicion.

"Like I started to say, before we began our trip down Memory Lane, you have to kill me. Within the next hour," she said. The way she said the words, so matter-of-factly, it sent a chill through me.

If she needed to die, then that was one thing. The far greater problem was how do you kill someone who is already dead?

***

Over the years, Harry and I have seen a lot of strange things. If people knew there were vampires, werewolves, monsters of every shape and kind, and aliens from planets too distant to be seen by Hubble, all walking among them, they would freak. But the ghost of my dead mother? That definitely ranked highest on my strange scale.

And it got even stranger when Mary explained she was the ghost of her future self. Twenty years in the future, to be exact. She apparently died after being in a coma for twenty years. A coma caused by being hit by a car, today.

Somehow, I was supposed to kill her so she wouldn't have to spend the next twenty years in a coma before she succumbed.

Russ Crossley

My head hurt. "Nope. I don't think so, Mom. Besides, why should I help you? I don't even like you!"

Mary hung her head. "Tell him, Harry."

Harry dropped his shoes to the floor with a thump. The odor of disturbed dust permeated the air. "She's right, Jimmy. She will be hit by the car today and be in the coma for twenty years…"

I felt Mary's dark eyes gazing at me. "Son. James. I am still your mother. I love you. I know I haven't been there for you for a long time." Her voice was gentle, enveloping me with its soft summer breeze quality.

"You bet your ass," I said. Even as I said the words, I knew I was being too harsh. What galled me most was she was right.

When I first met Harry in grade ten at John Oliver Secondary, he told me my whole life story in ten minutes. It was as if the guy worked for *Sixty Minutes*. Now here was my mother's damn ghost, confirming my best friend's twisted tale. Harry warned me there would be days like this. And Harry is never wrong.

"I'm so sorry, James. Sorry I wasn't there. Sorry I…" She paused. "I'm going to be hit by a car today. Then I'll be in a coma for the next twenty years before I die. The police will track you down as my only living relative, and you're going to tell them not to pull the plug on me. You're so consumed with guilt that you just can't let me go. I don't want you to go through that, son."

I glared at Harry, whose face was a shade of pink. He had never told me this about my mother. What good was a guy who left out the most important parts about a guy's mother? The messy bits, I call them.

He shrugged his broad shoulders. "Hey. Don't look at me. Sure, I saw her accident, and the coma thingy, but I thought you didn't wanta see her. I mean you always say…"

"Never mind," I cut him off. "We'll talk about this later."

Mary's ghost floated to the window over-looking the late morning traffic. Cars honked their horns and trucks rumbled by below our window. The odor of burnt gasoline wafted in from the street. She gazed into the street with a longing I had never seen in a living person, never mind a dead one.

Her voice became small. "I don't want to live the next twenty years of my earthly existence in a useless husk." She whirled to face me, her expression grim.

"You have to kill me."

What could I do? Harry said the car would hit her, and she is—or rather was—oh, shit—my head was spinning. I nodded. "Yeah, I guess so."

"Whoa," Harry said, holding his hands up as if he were surrendering to Castro's army. "You might be charged with murder. You can't just go around killing people, ya know. Besides, we don't know where Mary is right now."

I shot him a warning look. "Don't you start with me." I knew perfectly well that if I were going to be caught, Harry would know already. And somehow I knew that he knew I wouldn't be caught. (This stuff is just too weird for words.) He'd already seen it. Good thing neither of us have criminal minds or he and I would make a killing on horseracing or at the casinos. Honesty really does have its drawbacks.

Mary's ghost pointed out the window to the busy street. I moved to look where Mary was pointing. Sure enough, there, walking down the cracked sidewalk, was the very much alive Mary O'Shay, the former Mrs. Ivan Rusinski.

Harry and I looked at each other. He wore a stunned expression on his face, which I'm sure mirrored my own.

My mother had been this close to me and I had never even realized it.

I stood straight and looked at my partner. "So, Harry, how do I kill her?"

***

Mary's ghost told me she was only visible to Harry and me. And that she could have been visible to anyone she wanted to see her. She didn't want anyone else to see her but us at the moment. Strange how the rules of the paranormal so often turn out to be so simple.

Even more strange was that in some sort of cosmic joke, if we succeeded, then a woman would be murdered—this was really, really crazy.

We rode in silence in my '82 Buick. Mary sat—if that's what ghosts do—in the back seat, gazing around at the city that flashed by.

"I remember how this looked." An occasional glance in the rearview told me she was taking everything in with her strange eyes as we neared the suburb of New Westminster. The sparkling neon signs of the movie and entertainment complex known as Metropolis were behind us.

Mary's eyes were as wide as a child's as we passed the massive entertainment complex. "I don't remember this," she said in a tiny voice

Our destination beyond New West is Surrey.

It was nearly noon and the sun had warmed the inside of the ancient Buick. The faux leather seats stuck to my pants. I wasn't sure if it was the heat—or my nerves—making me sweat so profusely.

We arrived to find the sky train parking lot packed with cars.

The Eliminators

Not unusual at this time of day since the lot is for downtown commuters who save money by parking their cars here, then riding the rapid transit service to the downtown business district.

The parking lots were well known to cops and crooks alike as the car thief strip mall. Their new "owners" lined up every make and model of car and truck imaginable in neat rows ready for inspection.

When we arrived, we saw the bike patrol cop in her lemon-yellow vest with the word "POLICE" in bold black lettering on the back, pedaling away on her taxpayer funded thousand-dollar mountain bike. Perfect timing.

She didn't give us a second glance as she went by. Two guys in suits—regardless if the suits looked like their owners had slept in them—certainly weren't your usual car thief type. In normal circumstances she'd be right. But these were far from normal circumstances.

We drove slowly through the parking lot until we found an older model Toyota with button locks. It would be the easiest to steal.

I stepped out and used my telekinesis to unlock the driver's door. As I did so, Harry slid behind the wheel of the Buick.

Harry, his pale forehead beaded with sweat, motioned for me to hurry. His bloodless knuckles gripped the steering wheel. I had never seen him like this. His body trembled with nerves as he kneaded the plastic wheel as if he were making bread dough. My normally cool partner was scared. To tell the truth, so was I.

The door squealed metal-on-metal as I opened it. Harry squeezed his eyes tight. Damn!

I quickly sat behind the wheel and went to work on the steering column. I had stolen a couple of cars in my impetuous youth so I certainly knew how.

The plastic cover over the steering column came off easily and I managed to find the wires. I cut them with the box cutter I brought with me. I striped the wires and crossed them correctly. I twisted the yellow and blue wires together, then brought the green and white wires together to create the spark to kick over the starter motor.

Nothing. No spark.

Beads of sweat formed on my brow and dripped into my eyes, blinding me. I tried again. Nothing. I slammed the dashboard hard in frustration with my fist. Deciding I had wasted too much time, I stepped out, then realized the dashboard didn't look right. Someone had installed an after factory immobilizer.

I shook my head and silently chastised myself.

"What's the matter?" asked Harry, his voice an urgent whisper.

"Immobilizer. We have to find another car."

We started to cruise the lot again and quickly found an even older car. It was a pale green '72 Impala. Harry knew it because he'd owned one just like it in the late seventies.

A pig on gas, but it would more than do the job. The big V8 and the heavy steel body made it the perfect weapon.

***

Once back downtown, Mary directed us to the street she would be on this time of day. It was in Gastown, a tourist area of restored brick buildings and cobblestone streets named after Gassy Jack, a nineteenth-century bar owner and local rascal.

In the center of the area was an old steam clock. The cobblestones made for a bumpy ride, but the tourists thought the streets were quaint. To me it was just a jarring, joyless ride for the spine.

As we bumped over the worn cobblestones, my teeth rattled. Just great.

Harry parked the old Buick, now officially dubbed the "getaway car," on a side street while I would drive the Impala to the spot where Mary was going to be (at least according to our time-traveling ghost).

I would use the heavy car, run her down, and kill her. I was to make sure she was dead by backing up and running over her again.

We knew we'd be changing history, at least Mary's personal history. Of course, the history of the man who'd originally run her down would also be altered, in his case for the better.

What we knew for sure was a car would strike Mary; nothing could change that one fact. It might not be today, but it would happen. And she'd be in a coma if I didn't help her. To avoid countless years of silent suffering, she would die today by my hand.

I shook my head. I now knew what it felt to be Harry and I hated the pain in my belly. But I knew what I had to do. She'd begged me. And even after years of estrangement, she was still my mother.

Our plan meant I would abandon the Impala in an alley and escape in the Buick. Hopefully we would get away before anyone could identify us.

"Gotta do it fast," Mary said. "Like Al Pacino in the first *Godfather* movie when he shoots the gangster and the dirty cop."

Harry and I had forgone the usual PI baggy suits and ties, instead preferring to don jeans and tee shirts. In addition, I had added a New York Yankees ball cap and mirrored sunglasses. Harry, the Mr. GQ of our little firm, hated the disguises, but it would lessen the chances of being identified.

As I sat in the Impala, I felt my stomach churn.

A trace of bile invaded my mouth when I spotted the very much alive Mary O'Shay coming down the sidewalk toward me.

She looked happy. Doubt nearly forced me from the car to warn her about the other guy. But a greater fear of my own failure kept me glued to the seat. Harry said the accident was going to happen no matter what I did.

Mary would either die or be in a coma. What kind of choices were these? Why couldn't I just hit the guy who would hit her, and save her from the coma?

Harry said the only thing we could change was the time of Mary's accident, not the inevitability of it. Harry is always right.

My hands worried the steering wheel until I thought the pale green plastic would come off on my hands.

The vision of her being struck by the car became suddenly very clear in my mind. The scream. The blood. The sickening smack of her lifeless body hitting the pavement. I closed my eyes and struggled to push the sight and sounds of what was about to happen from my mind. And there was something else...

My eyes popped open as the passenger door flew open. It was Harry. "I'm with you, buddy."

"I know," I said. "Let's go."

The Impala moved easily into traffic. As I neared the crosswalk, I picked up speed. The cobblestones made the car bounce into the air as if it wanted to leave the ground.

The powerful engine roared and the wind rushed in through the open windows as we hurled toward my mother. There she was, frozen at the sight of the roaring pride of General Motors racing full speed toward her.

I closed my eyes and hit the accelerator hard. Harry screamed.

The Eliminators

I heard the slap of flesh landing hard as it pounded over the windshield of the car, followed by the screams of people on the street around us.

It happened so quickly I thought for a second I might have missed her, until I opened my eyes to glance in the rearview mirror. My heart leapt into my throat.

Framed by the mirror, in the middle of the street behind us, lay a crumpled human form. With both feet I slammed the brake pedal hard, causing us to be thrown violently forward. The air filled with the smell of burnt rubber and the screech of tires as we came to a stop. The seat belt holding me pressed against me until it hurt my chest.

I hit the shift lever into reverse, then stepped hard on the accelerator. The car raced backward over the prone lump lying in the middle of the street. It felt like we had hit a speed bump.

I stopped again, shifted into drive, then drove over the body for the last time and headed away. Out of the corner of one eye, I saw the shocked looks of the people watching the horrific spectacle.

Oh, my God. What have I done?

I steered the heavy car around a corner and then into a deserted alley. I felt as if I were moving in thick air as we climbed out of the car, leaving the doors open, and ran headlong down the dank, dirty alley. The sour smell of garbage, coming from the rusted steel dumpsters that lined the alley, assaulted my senses as we ran. Hot tears streamed down my cheeks.

I killed my own mother!

After what seemed like an eternity, we made it to the Buick and I threw my sunglasses to the street. Once inside, Harry started the car and we sped away.

He quickly reduced speed as cop cars and an ambulance screamed passed us, going in the opposite direction.

I glanced at Harry, tears blurring eyes that brimmed over with regret and grief. He shook his head sadly and I knew she was dead. I had not seen her for fifteen years and now she was dead.

I heard a soft voice behind me say, "It's OK, son. I know you love me."

***

The headline in the paper the next day stated a stolen car had killed an unidentified pedestrian in a crosswalk in Gastown. It was labeled a hit-and-run by the cops, probably—or so the reporter presumed—by kids joy riding. The cops said they would catch the culprits very soon. The article ended by saying the victim's name would not be released until the next of kin were contacted. Of course, I already knew the name.

Rain pelted the windows and the smell of fresh coffee permeated the tiny office. Harry's long legs were crossed, resting on his desk, his dark eyes were the saddest I had ever seen them. I felt numb.

"I guess Blakey's gonna be calling," murmured Harry.

"Yeah. I guess so."

"What we gonna tell him?"

I shrugged my shoulders. I had no idea. "If he asks, we'll tell him we were at a funeral."

"Yeah…" There was nothing else to say.

For several minutes the only sounds in our office came from the incessant ticking of the plastic battery-operated clock that hung off the wall. Finally, Harry said, "Where's the ghost?"

I sighed, then lifted my coffee mug with the Disney characters dancing happily across it to my lips. "She said she had to do something. But that she'd be here."

The room grew cold. "Hi, boys," said a cheery voice. Too cheery for a dead person in my reckoning.

"What the hell are you so happy about?" I asked, my voice as bitter as the overcooked coffee.

Mary chuckled. "I'm staying. I have permission."

I moved my legs off my desk and sat forward, my hands gripping the arms of my chair. "What the hell are you talking about?" I asked.

"I'm your new partner. I'm going to work cases with you boys."

Harry shook his head and snorted.

I thought about asking her who gave her permission, then decided against it. I didn't want to know.

This turn of events pretty much confirmed it: we are officially the strangest PI firm on the planet.

Now for a change of pace. A story about an alternate reality
where a lazy, good-for-nothing man is forced to save the human race,
and his wife, from certain doom.

End of the Flies

Russ Crossley

TONIGHT, JUST AS I SAT DOWN TO DINNER IN FRONT OF THE TV,
my wife, Merle, started screaming and running around the house.
Naturally, I ignored her.

This crazed behavior had been happening every couple of days
over the past month. I've tried a few times to assure her the sky
wasn't falling, but she just wouldn't believe me, so I gave up.

Then she ordered me to drop the newspaper I was reading. To
help me ignore her, I kept reading. Yes, I ignored her.

Why, you ask? Because she'd done this too many times and it
was driving me a little nuts.

Problem is, this time I should have paid a little more attention.
This time she was cursed up the ying-yang, and we (meaning all of
us) were in real trouble. Fortunately, some of what was upsetting her
managed to slip through my husband-filters.

Over the past month, she's told me stuff like the government
knows about a Texas-size meteor about to hit the Earth and wipe
us out, but they were withholding the information because we'd
all panic. If Texas really was about to land on my head, I know I'd
certainly be freaked out.

End of the Flies

This piece of paranoid crapola came from her hairdresser, an eighteen-year-old kid who read it on a conspiracy website.

Then there was the inevitable alien invasion. This came from her brother-in-law Albert before they carted him off to a rubber room upstate.

No, Seattle wasn't about to be invaded by little green men, or white sexless beings with big bald heads and eyes proportionally too big for their oval faces (whether they are male or female remains a mystery).

But today there was a new twist. Today she complained some guy calling himself Mope something (I don't recall the name exactly) walked into the mayor's office demanding the mayor let Mope's people go, or else.

His people? Who has people anymore? These days, not even a Wall Street banking executive claims they have people. (And if they do, they keep it on the QT.)

And what was this "or else" stuff? Since my wife is the executive assistant to the mayor, she's usually plugged into such things; but she had no idea what this Mope guy was talking about. And, she added, neither did Mayor Billy Ramses.

That was until the curse changed everything.

I flicked the channel changer to the five o'clock early news and turned up the sound. I was sitting with my TV dinner on the shaky, hollow aluminum TV tray in front of me, as usual. On the screen, the perfectly sprayed and combed channel two news anchor, Peter Hasting, the man with the perfect white teeth, started his newscast in the usual way.

For the past five years, he has always started with a flirty joke with the weather girl.

But today, for reasons that will become obvious, he suddenly froze in mid-punch-line and stared wide-eyed into the camera. His face actually changed to the color of wood ash. Not an easy task with all the makeup those guys pack on their kissers.

I've seen him use this particular dramatic tactic many times, to increase the suspense of the story to follow. I watched all this half-interested in this so-called Big News Development.

"We take you now to Lake Washington, where there is breaking news."

"What, no tagline? Come on, Pete, ol' buddy. Hook me, baby." I spoke at the television, then snorted in disgust before I stuffed a large forkful of greasy chicken strip into my mouth.

Peter's tone had that deadly earnestness reserved by local news anchors about to report the birth of a new cow to farmer Jones and family. *What a maroon.*

I glanced at Merle, seated to my left in her matching wing chair with her TV dinner on the tray in front of her. She hadn't touched her food. No loss there really, the chair probably tastes better.

I did think it odd that her cheeks were damp with tears and her hands were trembling. I rolled my eyes and turned my attention back to the television in time to see an aerial shot of the lake. It sure looked red. Strange. The sky visible in the background was still as blue as ever.

I chuckled around my mouthful of stringy chicken. "Hey, Merle. Will ya look at that? They broke out the helicopter to report the birth of a calf."

I shook my head, then crammed a forkful of the glutinous mashed potatoes with the artificial chicken gravy into my mouth. At least I wouldn't have to chew the stuff.

End of the Flies

I realized Merle was right not to eat this crap. I grunted and stuck my fork into the rubbery so-called bird meat, then shoved the tray away.

A dyed-blonde female reporter appeared on the screen standing on the lakeshore. "Thank you, Peter. This is Lori Oldsby, reporting from Lake Washington—"

I snatched the remote from the end table next to my chair and thumbed the off button. Lori and the crimson-colored lake disappeared into blackness.

I got up from the chair, stuffed my hands into the pockets of my tanned Dockers, and began to pace back and forth in front of Merle.

"Ya know, Merle, sometimes I wonder why we stay in this town. I mean, we eat TV dinners for supper every night. You work seven days a week for that walking penis of a mayor. And I'm in a dead-end job I hate. I mean, how long will it be before China takes over the aircraft manufacturing industry? Five years? Ten? Boeing can't last forever, ya know. We should move somewhere else."

"I'm cursed," Merle said softly.

I stopped pacing, placed my hands on my hips, and turned to face her. Strange. Why was her skin green? Maybe she wasn't feeling well.

"Are you OK?"

"I'm cursed," she repeated, only this time her voice had an edgy rasp to it. I must admit, it was kinda sexy actually.

"Oh, really? What is it this time? Aliens? The Loch Ness monster? Dracula? Zombies? What?" I snapped my mouth closed. I was shouting.

I crossed my arms over my chest and let out a breath. My frustration with the way she'd been acting for the past month had finally spilled over.

110

"Sorry." I closed my eyes and whispered, "It's just all this stuff you've been saying lately is driving me a little nuts and—" I opened my eyes and looked at Merle.

Oh, crap!

She was brilliant green, and a long, forked tongue flicked out of her mouth. I don't recall her having a long forked tongue, but it's surprising how a flicking tongue can be a real turn on, even when your wife is turning green.

"Ribit!" she croaked. Her body shape changed before my eyes. She was now sitting on her haunches like a dog. Or a frog…a frog! My wife had become a frog!

"What's going on here?" I glared at the frog. "What have you done with my wife, hoppy?"

The frog responded with a deep croak again, then leapt off the chair, leaving behind a pile of Merle's clothes. Now my wife the frog was jumping around our living room naked. What if someone else came into the room right now?

I slapped my forehead with the palm of my hand. What was the matter with me? My wife is a frog, for goodness' sake. A frog.

My eyes narrowed. This had to be the work of that Mope guy she talked about earlier. This had to be the "or else."

But how do I find him? I certainly wanted my Merle back. And just to be clear, Merle the human, not Merle the frog.

***

After I picked up Merle and put her in the cab of my pickup, I drove to city hall. Along the way I passed groups of frogs. They were everywhere. In the designer clothing shops, coffee shops, dry cleaners, hairdressers, jewelry stores, book stores.

111

End of the Flies

Everywhere. But the weird thing was that there were men frantically trying to catch them. Every time they managed to catch a frog, it slipped out of their hands and jumped away.

What was going on? Had the whole world gone frog-centric? Was there a frog convention in town? Now *I* was being paranoid. When your wife turns into a frog, it sure messes you up.

Then it hit me like a foul ball at a Mariners' game: there were no women on the streets. Only men and frogs.

Like my Merle, had all the women changed into frogs? But why frogs? Was this Mope guy responsible? Or was it someone or something else? Was it aliens, or swamp gas, or a government experiment gone wrong?

I certainly didn't know. All I had right now were questions. I only hoped her boss, Mayor Ramses, would have some answers.

When I arrived at city hall, the guards who were normally at the entrance to the visitor parking lot had disappeared. As I passed the guard shack, I noticed two uniforms lying in heaps on the floor, as if the guards had stripped them off and dropped them right there.

I pulled into an empty stall in the lot and turned off the engine.

"Ribit!" Merle croaked at me from the seat beside me.

"Yup, we're here, babe. Don't worry, I'm gonna find a way to make you human again, or my name isn't Rusty T. Quits."

A fly that had been trapped in my truck flew by Merle. Her dark eyes followed the path of the insect, then suddenly her long tongue flicked out of her wide mouth and snatched the fly in midflight. And just like that, the fly disappeared inside her mouth.

"Ribit," she croaked again. She seemed happy to have the bite-sized snack, but I was horrified.

Oh, crap. When she gets normal again, how am I going to tell her she ate a fly with her tongue?

I keep a canvas tool bag in the bed of my truck in a locked box. I got out of the cab, with Merle resting on the flat of one hand. I then climbed into the flatbed and unlocked the steel box. I emptied the tools from the bag and carefully placed Merle inside. She didn't protest or try to jump away. I thought about saying, "Good frog," but it would just sound stupid and condescending to a woman in her condition.

Still, her big black eyes gazed at me seemingly trustingly. Before I zipped the bag shut, I assured her everything would be fine, though I had serious doubts.

"Hey, pal, you talkin' to the frog?" said a man's voice behind me.

I slowly turned around to discover a man with hair the color of snow dressed in all white from his shoes to his suit jacket. The corners of his mouth were curled slightly upward. Was he mocking me? I hate being mocked.

I scowled uneasily. "Like, yeah. I'm married to the frog, so watch what you're saying about her, pal." My day had gone so badly I wasn't about to take any crap from anyone, and especially not from a guy who sells garbage bags for a living. Not even if they're good garbage bags.

Now he smiled. "Sorry. No offense meant. It's just that I've met a lot of people today married to frogs, or their girlfriends are frogs, or their best friends are frogs." The smile disappeared. "It's been a strange day."

I nodded, then stopped and studied him for a second or two. "Who are you, anyway? I've been to city hall many times, and I would remember you."

Both of his white eyebrows rose on his forehead. "Oh, do you work here?"

"No. My wife does." I stuck one hand in the pocket of my Dockers and picked up the tool bag with the other. "Well, she did until…you know." I sighed. "Somehow I don't think they'll keep her on as the executive assistant to Mayor Ramses now that she's a frog."

"Mayor Ramses," blurted the garbage bag man, suddenly excited. "Your wife works, sorry, I mean worked, for the mayor?"

"Uh, yeah, sure…why?"

He came up to me and draped a long arm across my shoulders and began to guide me to the steps leading to the lobby doors.

"My friend, you and I can do each other some good."

"Who are you, anyway?" I asked again.

He chuckled. "Teamsters, Local 4402, Sorcerers, Magicians, and Spirits Union. I'm the organizer for Moe Sheppard. Jacob's the name. I'm his right-hand man. Your wife ever speak of us?"

I shook my head. "No, not really." The guy behind this was named Moe, not Mope. What an idiot I am. I had gained new respect for my frog…uh, I mean my wife.

But, magicians? Sorcerers? If my Merle ever became human again, I'd never doubt any of her crazy conspiracy theories, not ever.

"So you know this Mope—I mean, Moe—guy who threatened the mayor?" I asked hopefully.

We were just outside the twin glass doors to the city hall lobby. We stopped short, too short, and I nearly fell forward, but he held me tightly. I'd annoyed him.

The last thing I wanted to do was piss off a magician, or whatever he was. I could be the next one turned into a frog, or something worse, like a rat or a pig. I couldn't imagine spending the rest of my days wallowing in garbage and mud.

114

Jacob's arms dropped to his sides and he frowned at me. "The teamsters union has no knowledge of any threats, real or imagined, ever being expressed or implied to anyone."

"OK, OK, let's not go all Senate-Investigation. It's just two good ol' boys talkin'. I'm only repeating what Merle told me."

Jacob's eyes narrowed. "Who's Merle?"

I rolled my eyes. "My wife. Like I said, she's a frog, but I love her, warts and all. She's my frog."

Jacob grinned. "Of course she is. No worries, pal." Somehow I'd become his pal again. "Let's go inside and meet with the mayor and Moe. They're in talks right now."

I studied him. I didn't trust the guy. He seemed a little too slick, like a used car salesman. But then again, what did I have to lose? And maybe I could talk this Moe guy into making Merle human again.

I shrugged. "Yeah, OK. Lead on, Macduff."

He looked at me quizzically, like a dog when it's confused. I'd found his Achilles heel. He didn't comprehend

"It's an expression meaning take me to your leader," I explained.

Jacob shook his head. "OK, if you say so."

I smiled to myself and followed him through the glass doors into the carpeted lobby. Score one for the janitor.

***

We entered the mayor's office without knocking to find Moe and Billy Ramses silently glaring at each other from opposite sides of the mayor's large, glass-topped desk. There wasn't anything on the desk between them, not even a scrap of paper, never mind the computer monitor I'd seen on Billy's desk the last time I was here.

End of the Flies

As I recall, that was about a month ago, just before Merle started her conspiracy rants. At that moment I could have kicked myself for not believing her.

"Hey, Billy," I greeted the mayor as I set the tool bag on his desk. He glanced at me and nodded without saying anything in return. It was like watching a staring contest or drying paint.

Billy's jowly features were pasty and his chipmunk cheeks were ruddy. His blood pressure must be about ready to explode.

Moe looked over at me. His arms and face were deeply tanned and his build was reminiscent of an NFL quarterback. Six feet four inches of solid muscle, with a dimple at the end of a wide chin; he sure intimidated me.

I've always pictured magicians as gnarled, stoop-shouldered old men who wore pointy hats and flowing robes, so this guy was a complete surprise. So much for the Hollywood cliché.

I offered to shake his hand by sticking out mine.

Moe smiled at me and stood. He took my hand in his and I was glad when he didn't squeeze too hard. I winced and struggled to not show the pain. The triumphant look in his eyes told me I'd failed. He released my hand and let it drop to my side. The circulation would come back, eventually.

"Hi. Moe Sheppard," he said, introducing himself. I couldn't place the accent. Maybe he was Icelandic. I'd never met an Icelandian before.

"Uh, Rusty T. Quits."

"Tquits? Is that French?"

"No, it's T period Quits," I explained, "and it's Polish, on my father's side."

He smiled. "So you come from a family of Quitters is that it?"

I was beginning to take a serious dislike to this guy and I'd just met him. "No, we're Quakers, actually. We don't believe in violence." I looked him straight in the eyes. "But there have been exceptions."

He smiled smugly. I wanted to slap him, but since he out weighted me by at least thirty pounds of muscle, I decided to let it go.

"What can I do for you, Quits?" he asked.

"I'd like to talk to Billy. Privately."

Moe shrugged. "Sure, why not? Me and Mayor Stall-tactic have been getting nowhere. Maybe you can talk some sense into him."

Moe and Jacob left us, saying they were going to the cafeteria to get some lunch. They'd be back in twenty minutes.

Once we were alone, I sat in a chair across the desk from a weary Billy Ramses. "Billy, tell me what's going on around here. All the women in town have been turned into frogs." I opened the tool bag and Merle jumped out to land on the desk.

"Ribit," she croaked, and blinked repeatedly under the glare of the florescent lights.

"Get that thing off my desk," said Billy, raising his voice an octave.

"Billy, this is Merle."

"Oh." He collapsed back into his leather executive chair, a defeated man. He undid the top button of his white dress shirt and loosened his red striped tie.

"They want me to let their people go," he said, bitterly. His eyes were locked on his desk.

"People? What people, and where are they going?"

He looked up at me, his brow creased.

"The union wants the city to pay for two weeks in Hawaii every year for all their members. I can't agree to that. The taxpayers would lynch me."

"And who would that be, exactly—the frogs, or the husbands of the frogs?"

As if a lightbulb had suddenly gone off, his features relaxed. "Ya know, I never thought of that." He reached into his suit jacket pocket and pulled out his cell phone. "I should call my wife."

"You mean your frog?"

He stopped, his index finger hovering over the numbers on his phone. "Ya know, I never thought of that, either."

I wondered how this moron ever got elected. "Billy, what you have to do is agree to their terms and get back your wife and mine and the rest of the taxpayers. It's the only way. OK?"

"I could nuke 'em," he said.

I shook my head. "No, Billy, only the president can order that, and besides, who ya gonna nuke, union headquarters?"

"Oh. Ya know—"

"You never thought of that, either?" I finished.

He nodded sheepishly.

***

A few days later at home in my living room, I watched the five o'clock news snuggled together with Merle on a new loveseat. (Human Merle that is, not frog Merle).

Peter Hasting was speaking. "Alien space ships have landed in Washington. Preliminary reports are they are demanding we turn over all potatoes…"

I reached for the remote and turned him off. As the screen went dark, I looked at Merle. "What do ya think?"

"Anything's possible," she said.

I nodded.

Her brow wrinkled.

"What is it?" I asked.

"Have you ever had hunger cravings for something weird?"

"You mean like flies?"

"Yeah. Weird, huh?"

I smiled. Yeah, if I hadn't convinced Billy to give in to the union's demands, it would have been the end of the flies for sure.

I only hoped Moe and Jacob were enjoying Hawaii.

This alternate history story postulates a very different United States than the one we know. In this reality, dark forces helped the South win the Civil War. One woman is determined to stop this pestilence from spreading over the entire world, even if it means sacrificing someone she loves.

Unnatural Immortal

Russ Crossley

IN MID-AUGUST, NIGHTS IN THE TALL TIMBERS FOREST are muggy and stifling, the air thick as pudding. But the tranquility of this green meadow in the middle of these elegant pines and majestic oaks provided a welcome respite for Amy Selkirk, who sat almost buried in the long, wild grasses tipped yellow by the sun. Leaning back, she rested her weight on her hands, relishing the peace and quiet of the dark woods surrounding her. But even the meadow's tranquility could do little to lessen the oppressive humidity of the summer and the danger that lurked around every tree.

She was bathing in this fleeting escape from the real world.

Amy lolled her head back with her eyes closed, dreaming of her revenge while the sweet odor of wildflowers filled her nostrils, the fragrant jasmine and lavender providing a pleasant distraction. In reality, she was unable to fully relish the peace this place of retreat promised for very long.

The unquenchable thirst gripping Amy's every waking hour was like a massive weight pressing on her by some unseen force.

Unnatural Immortal

Too often these days the hunger for blood pushed away all other thoughts. Each passing day this need became more intense, threatening to consume her. Soon Amy's humanity would disappear, completely lost in a swirling vortex of lust and death that had become her new reality.

Time was growing short.

Her sire, Argos, the vampire who made her one of the undead, had preyed on her weaknesses and insecurity, using them as weapons to take control of her and her sister by offering her immortality. She had agreed to become a vampire before she realized her romantic notions of immortality were false, the truth far more terrible than she imagined and far from romantic. Argos had tricked her into this existence of living death.

Early on after her transformation, she struggled with her decision to challenge her sire until she came to realize Argos was a power-mad despot bent on building his own personal empire on the bloody, broken bodies of human cattle—the ultimate goal being his quest for absolute power. He had to be stopped before he enslaved the world to his will, and Amy was determined to destroy him before it was too late.

Sighing, she opened her eyes and turned her head slightly to look at the corpse, her prey, in the inky blackness of the night lying facedown buried in the grass next to her.

Amy had laid him next to her after carrying him across her shoulders up the hill to this meadow. His name was Edward Lamp; he had been a plantation owner from the nearby town of Andersonville.

The late Mr. Lamp bought his cotton from slave owners, men who exploited what she still thought of as her people. Slavery was an abomination that also had to end.

Amy was determined to scour this inhuman practice from the face of the earth. Lamp would be the first of many who would die before her mission in this world ended.

Argos and her sister, Mary, must die if she was to save humanity from a terrible fate.

After arriving from Europe, Argos had made his fortune in the new world by growing cotton on the plantation he stole from its former owner after that owner disappeared under mysterious circumstances. Fellow plantation owners readily accepted Argos' explanation that the previous owner had fled to Europe after failing to make good on his debts. Argos generously paid for the man's passage back to his homeland and he assumed his plantation in exchange. Of course, these so-called facts were completely false. Amy knew Argos had killed the previous owner, burying the head and torso separately in his own cotton field.

Argos then had a copious supply of the fresh, iron-rich blood supplied by the many slaves on his plantation, but also from slaves of nearby farms. It also meant the number of vampires was growing exponentially all across the Confederate States of America, also known as the CSA, with Argos at the epicenter of death and terror.

Amy intended to control the supply of fresh victims from the source and restore the world to balance. At least as she saw balance.

In order for her plan to work, every existing vampire would have to be permanently dead. As a one-woman army, she had the impossible task of tracking and killing all Argos' victims and their spawn. It reminded her of trying to stop ripples in a pond after dropping in a pebble. She needed help, which meant she needed a plan.

First she must build her own vampire army. Edward Lamp would be the tenth member of this army.

Her concern was it had been over one hundred fifty years since
the Union failed to stop the Confederate States from over-running
the country, so she had very real doubts about her own ability to stop
Argos by herself when an entire nation had failed.

A more personal challenge she had to overcome was her
remaining human aversion to taking human life. She abhorred killing
the living.

Amy shivered at the memory of Argos sinking his fangs into her
flesh, the wet sound of him puncturing her skin, his fangs tearing
through the soft tissue of her neck, then the pain as they sank into
an artery in order to drink her blood. She recalled the exhilarating
mix of pain, ecstasy, and horror than ran through her as her lifeblood
ebbed.

She also recalled the finality of the fading sight of the filthy room
she shared with her sister Mary when the release of death finally
enveloped her. At the time, it seemed good to die.

The next thing she remembered was the warm, coppery taste of
blood passing between her lips and the musty scent of iron in her
nostrils. When she finished drinking her prey's thick life force, Amy
sat back on her haunches on the straw mattress to discover, to her
horror, she had killed her beloved sister.

Mary's stare at her with unseeing eyes still haunted her. Mary's
motionless form, not breathing, a pale, waxy apparition, the side of
whose neck was a ragged mess of torn skin, veins, and the oozing
red wounds where Amy's fangs had ripped Mary's flesh was fresh in
Amy's memory.

Gripped by the shock and horror of what she had done, Amy
grabbed handfuls of her own hair and ripped them out, then threw
back her head as a scream ripped from her lungs.

Her body was wracked by deep, bone-shattering sobs as salty thick tears began to stream down her cheeks forming muddy rivulets on her cold, dead skin.

Yes, Amy would never forget Mary's ugly death until, in what seemed like only minutes but could have been hours or even days, her sister gasped and began to breath once again. Amy watched Mary's breaths coming in short gasps as the wounds closed around tiny, round scabs of healing flesh. Mary's undead eyes slowly opened to reveal yellow eyes like those of a cat. Then her lips parted to reveal elongated incisors.

Mary licked her lips as her eyes narrowed and her once-dead gaze focused on Amy. "Hello, sister, should we feed?"

Amy realized immediately her beloved sister had become like Argos and herself. She had made Mary an undead monster spawned from hell. Her sister's death was on Amy's head. Now it was Amy's responsibility to end her beloved sister's immortality.

Unlike her sister, Amy had chosen to become a vampire. Her free will had resulted in a living death until the end of time.

Amy could have simply allowed the sun to dissolve her dead flesh, but so far she'd been unable to take her own life. What little humanity remained within her didn't want to die, not completely.

The irony was that once her humanity disappeared, the need to kill would be all she would lust after. All thoughts of her former life would be overwhelmed and she'd no longer be human. She'd witnessed these phenomena before.

Amy closed her eyes and shuddered at the image of the inhuman monsters she'd seen wandering the grounds of the plantation at night. Argos forbade his minions to attack his slave stock, but his neighbor's slaves were fair game.

Many slaves were reported missing but the humans assumed they had run off—a not uncommon occurrence with all the abusive plantation owners.

Posses of heavily armed men had been organized to locate the missing slaves, but so far none had been found.

Amy smirked to herself. She knew where Argos' prey slept during the day, but the humans would never believe her if she told them. After all, she was just another slave and vampires were a myth. The other still-human slaves thought she was a voodoo woman, so they avoided her as if she had the plague.

The buzz of an air patrol not far away and coming from the direction of the Hoover Mountains made her tense and sucks in a breath. Her eyes shot open and she shifted her gaze to look at Edward Lamp, still lying prone on the grass. Lamp hadn't been resurrected yet and there was no telling how long it would be before he arose.

This could be a problem.

Using her ability to see in the dark as if it were midday, Amy scanned the stands of trees ringing the perimeter of the meadow. She grunted when she found the perfect spot. A cave in the side of a hill would be the perfect place to store Lamp until he was resurrected. Amy would need him and she wasn't about to let the CSA police have him, not when her plans were so close to nearing fruition.

Grabbing Lamp's body, she tossed him over her left shoulder and carried him to the cave. Just after they entered the cover of the cave, a beam of white light lit up the meadow as if it were midday rather than two in the morning, forcing Amy to cover her eyes with her arms. The real sun would rise in just over three hours so she hoped the air patrol would have moved on well before then.

"Amy Selkirk," said an amplified voice, "we know you're there. Reveal yourself."

Doubts invaded Amy's consciousness, causing her to hesitate. How had they found her? She had been careful to mask her movements and hiding places during the daylight hours. Maybe someone saw her take Edward Lamp?

If she failed to respond, no doubt the CSA police would begin carpet-bombing the meadow. The bombs would definitely kill her but would also destroy Edward's corpse and she needed him. The world needed him alive until the rebellion ended. Argos was the eye of this hurricane of terror. He would be the last to be destroyed, then vampirism would end forever and the CSA would be finally defeated.

"Turn off the light and I'll come out," Amy said, shouting to be heard over the roar of the air car's twin turbines that held it aloft on a cushion of air.

The pilots must have heard her because the searchlight blinked out leaving only the craft's soft, indigo running lights to illuminate the meadow.

The air car then floated to the ground, landing on its tripod undercarriage, the engines' roar quickly diminishing, then stopping altogether as the craft came to rest on the grass.

The side cargo door swung upward on hydraulic arms accompanied by the soft whir of the motors. Immediately two armed CSA police troopers burst out onto the squashed grass, dressed in head to foot gray and green battle armor, their faceplates closed, their automags scanning the area around them ready to fire on anyone foolish enough to attack.

From bitter experience, Amy knew the troopers' weapons were loaded with rounds that would shred her into fleshy ribbons of bloody meat that even her ability to heal would be useless against. The CSA had learned the most efficient method to destroy a vampire without holy water or wooden stakes. Those ancient weapons against the undead were a thing of the past. Why risk close and personal? Why not kill from a safe distance?

Amy shuddered as she recalled several friends who had been shredded by CSA weapons, their flesh peeling off their bones, then burned to ash as she watched in horror. And Argos standing beside her, a sly grin on his lips as his police force murdered her friends. The choking stench of burnt flesh still filled her nostrils, accompanied by the wisps of charred remains carried by the wind, created by the swirling fires that seemed to invade every orifice of her body and cling to her clothing for days after.

Amy's eyes flitted to Lamp, who had yet to arise; then she stumbled out of the cave mouth, walking toward the two heavily armed police troopers with their weapons trained on her.

Her breath caught in her throat when she saw Argos, dressed in his usual head-to-toe black clothing. His shoulder-length, slick, shiny black hair was pulled into a tight ponytail revealing his angular features. He stepped out of the air car with her sister by his side. Mary's yellow eyes glinted in the running lights of the air car.

"Mary?" Amy said after coming up short. Her heart beat hard and her hands trembled. The old fears and doubts resurfaced from deep within her.

Amy had sworn revenge when she learned Argos had planned from the beginning to make her change her sister into one of the undead.

And she vowed to free her sister from the curse she had inflicted on her. Argos detested love in all its forms, even between siblings. His intention all along had been to make an example of the two sisters to the rebellious slaves by having Amy curse her beloved sister, Mary, with vampirism, demonstrating anyone could be made to turn on anyone, even their own beloved ones.

A knot of pure hatred burned within Amy as Argos, with a knowing smile on his thin, bloodless lips, his manner cocky, approached. Her hands formed fists at her sides and she fought the urge to strike out at the bastard.

"Hello, my dear," he said in his deep voice as he and Mary drew near.

Amy wanted to tear him open and gut him like a melon but she held back when a furtive glance at the troopers confirmed they still had their weapons trained on her. They'd burn her down before she could finish one step toward their master. She knew they were also vampires, so their reflexes would be as good as her own.

"Hello, Argos," she said, her eyes shifting to look at Mary's ash gray face, then back to lock eyes with Argos. She was determined not to show him any fear or surrender to his will. With herculean effort, Amy had thus far managed to retain a portion of her humanity, making it difficult for Argos to control her, and she vowed to never let him control her or anyone else again.

But she also knew eventually her free will would disappear with her humanity. She fought against his power as much as she was able, but being this close to him chipped away at her inner defenses like a pick at a block of ice.

Argos reached into the pocket of his knee-length black pea coat and withdrew an ivory pipe.

Placing the tip between his lips, he extracted a shiny, gold-plated lighter from his other pocket and after lighting it used the yellow flame to light the tobacco in the bowl of the pipe. He puffed and the contents glowed as smoke rose from the pipe. Amy could smell the rum-soaked tobacco.

After putting the lighter back in his coat pocket, he placed his free hand behind him and stared at her, puffing on his pipe, his inky gaze studying her. A sense of unease grew inside Amy with each passing second of silence.

Finally he spoke. "So we seem to have reached an impasse, my dear Amy. I gave you what you asked for and then you betrayed me. Is this the way for one of my children to garner my favor?"

Amy snorted. "You made me kill my sister...turn her into a monster..." Her voice disappeared behind a wall of rising anger.

Argos' brow furrowed and his eyes became hard. He tapped out his pipe into the grass, some of the embers still glowing, then placed it back in his coat pocket. She could sense his seething anger. "Amy, you're planning an insurrection against me. That is a violation of my trust and very disappointing."

Amy froze, startled by his words. She realized he should have killed her as soon as she appeared from the cave but he hadn't. Why?

"I should be dead...we all should be..."

"I think you know better than to say such a thing to me." Argos moved closer to her, giving the impression of him swooping down on her as if he were a bird of prey, which in a sense he was.

Amy took a step backward but in her mind she decided to stand firm. She glanced at her sister, who had an expression of wonder on her face that mingled with fear in her eyes. Then Amy looked back at her now furious former master.

It occurred to her that his anger made him weak; he had not realized he had stepped within her kill zone. She was about to throw caution to the wind and launch herself at Argos, intending to tear out his throat, when a man's voice from behind her caused her to hesitate.

'What's going on out here?" It was Edward Lamp, finally resurrected from death.

Argos stepped out of Amy's range as his features relaxed. "Nothing of consequence, my dear friend." His deep voice was heavy with sarcasm. "You are just in time to see me deal with a traitor."

Amy turned her head to look at Lamp. "He means I'm a traitor for not buying into his plans to change the entire world into his personal vampire army with him as absolute ruler."

Lamp, a big man over six feet tall, with broad shoulders and muscular arms, smirked. His thick body was now primed with the additional physical strength that came with becoming a vampire. He strode across the meadow, his wide face becoming more serious with each step. Finally he stood between the two armed troopers. He swept them both off their feet with his massive arms. They landed hard on their backs and lay still as their guns slipped from their grasps.

"I may have just changed the odds," he said, grinning at Amy.

Amy's eyes narrowed as she shifted her gaze to Argos, whose eyes were wide. This was something he hadn't expected.

Instead of fighting them, Argos turned and ran for the air car, which had already started its engines. It took off as soon as Argos had leapt aboard, the door closing behind him.

Coward, thought Amy.

Unnatural Immortal

"Thank you, Lamp," she said, turning to face her newly minted creation. "I'm sorry I turned you, but as you saw, it was necessary." Or at least she hoped he realized the severity of the situation.

At the end of the day, Lamp would have either been made a vampire by her or by Argos. It seemed he appreciated her cause, especially seeing how Argos had reacted to his sudden appearance.

"So what is the deal between you and Argos?" Amy asked Lamp as she moved to wrap one arm around her sister's shoulders. Amy was pleased when Mary didn't flinch but instead pressed her body against Amy's side.

Lamp emitted a deep-throated chuckle. "I've never liked the son of a bitch. More than once I threw him off my land when I caught him sniffing around my slave huts."

Amy's stomach tightened at his use of the word slave. She'd momentarily forgotten this man had been as despicable as any owner of enslaved human beings.

The grin slowly faded from Lamp's square-jawed features as his expression became serious and his eyes narrowed. "I knew what he was and I wasn't about to let him take any of my workers. I treated them well and protected them from the bloodsuckers as best I could." He shrugged slightly, then continued. "Argos swore to kill me but every time he appeared I managed to drive him off. I used fire, wooden stakes, crosses, garlic...everything at my disposal to stop him." His brow furrowed. "Of course, now that I'm one of you, I don't know if I'll be able to continue protecting my people."

Amy's breath caught in her throat and her heart seemed to skip a beat. "What do you mean, your people?"

"I'm one quarter black on my grandmother's side. I inherited the plantation and vowed to treat the workers fairly and pay them. So far I've been able to keep my promise."

Amy's mind whirled with uncertainty and doubt. He could be lying. She had never heard of a plantation owner in the CSA paying slaves. Why had she not heard of this? "You're lying," she said, firmly convinced her words were true.

Lamp's wide face reflected his anger and his large, meaty hands formed fists. "No, I'm not." Amy watched as the anger in his eyes slowly faded, his features relaxed, and his fists unclenched. "I had to keep what I was doing secret or the other plantation owners would have told my buyers, who would have had me blacklisted. Not that I'm that concerned about money, but the loss for my workers would be far more than my personal fortunes would be able to afford." He sighed and turned his back to her as a breeze sprang up carrying with it the scent of the pine trees north of the meadow.

What Lamp was saying actually made sense. Amy made a decision knowing time was growing short. Argos wasn't about to let her get away again. He would end this once and for all—as far as he was concerned, at least.

"Lamp—"

Lamp turned back to face her with a grin on his lips, his gray eyes sparkling. "Call me Ed; everyone does."

Amy smiled to herself. She had taken a liking to this big man. "OK, Ed. I'm going to stay here with my sister. I urge you, beg you, actually, to continue the fight I started to destroy Argos."

Ed Lamp didn't say anything for several seconds, his eyes flitting between her and Mary. "What about you two?"

"Argos has no doubt ordered this area to be carpet bombed. In fact, I don't think you've got much time to make it to safety before a fleet of air cars arrives. Mary and I will stay behind and act as decoys so you can get away."

133

His words suggested he'd agree, but Amy needed to know for sure. "Ed. Will you do as I ask?"

Ed's eyes became hard and he nodded, his mouth a grim line of determination. Amy was satisfied.

As if to confirm his acceptance of her mission, he then stepped up to take her right hand in his. "I wish you well in the next world." His now sad eyes shifted to Mary, then back to her. "Both of you."

With those final words, Ed Lamp released her hand and ran toward the tree line, soon disappearing into the darkened, tangled forest of trees beyond.

Amy watched until Ed was out of sight and she couldn't hear him in the brush any more, then turned to focus her attention on Mary. Moving to stand in front of her sister, Amy put her hands on Mary's shoulders.

"What are we going to do?" asked Mary, her eyes curious.

A single tear ran from Amy's left eye down her cheek. "My unnatural immortal, I'm about to release you from the curse." Amy swallowed hard. "But don't worry, we'll see each other again soon." The iron scent of Mary's tainted blood filled her nostrils as she bent closer to her sister's ivory-skinned neck, steeling herself to deliver the killing bite.

"Oh," was Mary Selkirk's last word as Amy sank her fangs into her sister's neck and ended her undead existence.

Her sister's body sagged in her arms as air escaped Mary's lungs for the last time; the sound was quickly drowned out by the roar of multiple turbines that shattered the meadow's tranquility. The police fleet of air cars had arrived to bomb them into the next world.

Amy's heart was finally at peace as the bombs began to fall, secure in the knowledge Ed Lamp would exact revenge for not only her but for the countless people suffering from the curse placed on them by Argos and his undead horde.

Zombies abound in various media today because, with stories in the news about impending deadly pandemics, end of the world stories have once again become part of popular culture. Such stories go back to the earliest days of speculative fiction. This exciting tale is set in a possible future where secret operatives are determined to stop a zombie plague at its source—or die trying.

Dragon Rising

Russ Crossley

"GARGOYLE, THIS IS DRAGON. OVER." The stealth drone hovering in the night sky high above the streets of Vancouver boosted her COM signal so she could communicate with command. Without the signal boost, her ability to contact the on-duty controller would be sporadic at best.

"Go ahead, Dragon, this is Gargoyle. Over."

She spoke softly into the mike in her helmet. "Current readings show grid reference 1-5 is deserted. Permission to move to grid reference 1-6."

"Acknowledged. Permission granted. Good hunting, Dragon. Gargoyle out."

Jesse Splint lowered her arm, resting her gloved palm on the butt of the silenced nine-millimeter pistol in the holster on her hip. Her mouth was dry, but she ignored her own physical needs. The mission was too important, hydration could wait. The future depended on her successfully discovering the source of the outbreak.

Jesse stole a peek around the corner of the damp, slime-coated brick wall of the dank alley. The rain-slicked pavement and the dark, quiet, seemingly deserted office towers were all she could see through the night vision ocular units in her helmet. She was unable to detect movement: human, animal, or, thankfully, the presence of any undead.

Two hours wasn't a lot of time to complete her mission but that was all she'd been given. She had to move fast.

If she failed she might end up dead, or perhaps undead, but hers was, after all, a high-risk profession. Her breathing was steady, and according to the heads-up display in her helmet, her heart rate and blood pressure were well within the normal range. The helmet also displayed the current time and date. A countdown indicator had been added so she was aware of the looming deadline.

One hour, fifty minutes.

Time had become her enemy.

To the untrained eye, the streets of the central core of Vancouver appeared deserted, but she knew better. Recent intelligence reports stated the undead lurked around every corner and in every abandoned building. If at all possible, she'd stay in the streets and avoid entering any of the buildings. Staying in the open meant less chance of being cornered by a herd of zoms.

Not that she was afraid; danger was her chosen profession, her calling. Something her late father never understood when she'd reluctantly told him she was joining Special Operations. She had known how he'd react when she dropped out of medical school, but it was her life and she wanted to serve humanity in her own way. She craved action, not test tubes.

Jesse brought the sensor unit screen on the armband on her left arm to eye level.

A red dot on the six-by-two-inch display represented the stealth drone high over the downtown core. It had stopped moving, meaning the device had completed its sweep. The readings confirmed what her eyes were telling her. Being dependent on machines was a curse as far as she was concerned. Machines were unreliable. Your buddy next to you was a better safety net than any machine ever built. Too bad she was alone, but since she had insisted on a solo recon, any consequences were hers alone.

She'd been dropped behind the security corridor less than half an hour ago and so far hadn't seen any signs of life or movement of any kind. At the mission intelligence briefing, she had been told the inner core of the decimated city was crawling with undead. They should be everywhere, yet the evidence so far suggested otherwise. What else had intelligence missed? Her jaw tightened. Had she been discovered?

Jesse moved quickly and as quietly as possible down the deserted alley until she came to the junction with the street. Checking the sensor display again, she determined grid 1-6 was located half a klick west of her current position.

Rain had begun to fall. Traces of the chemical odor in the rainwater made it through the stealth suit's filters, wrinkling her nose. She'd never enjoyed the smell of unfiltered water and was thankful she lived under the dome protecting new Seattle. At least in Seattle the water was safe to drink and the food plentiful.

Making sure to stay close to the ivy-covered forty-story buildings, she hurried toward the new grid coordinates. The area she was heading for was at the intersection of Burrard and Hastings Streets. Jagged tears from minor yet frequent earthquakes fractured the worn, sagging asphalt.

Dragon Rising

The once smooth cement sidewalks were split by the roots of untended trees planted decades ago, their root systems expanding and destroying man's work. Knots of weeds and wild grasses inhabited the cracks.

Once at the junction of the two main streets, she could see the old harbor and the two convention centers. Intelligence suspected one of the two convention centers was the epicenter of the infection.

Evidence extracted from a captured undead—designated zombie-alpha—was tested. In the thing's cells, the science team discovered minute traces of seawater and pigeon excrement. After the death of the human population in Vancouver, upwards of ten thousand pigeons had settled in and around the convention centers. No one knew why exactly, but the speculation was the birds were flocking to a food source at the site. Again, no one knew why, and while the drones confirmed the sudden increase in bird population, no amount of machine surveillance discovered the reasons for this behavior.

Jesse knew boots-on-the-ground Intel was best when you needed answers to tough questions. Her theory was that someone was manufacturing zombies from spare body parts. Sure, it was pure speculation and too horrible to contemplate, but she believed her theory had merit. Her current mission would finally confirm her suspicions.

Her degree in advanced paranormal studies at the Special Operations Academy often made her a target for ridicule by the close-minded in SOB. Muscle heads, she mused. Brute force was all they understood.

Besides, she didn't need the brass's spotlights on her. The truth was, she hoped and prayed she was wrong—dead wrong.

Moving quickly along the empty street, she occasionally ducked into an alley and held her breath, straining for any stray sounds registering in the audio sensors in her helmet. But the only noise the sensors detected was the steady patter of rain bouncing off the wet pavement. The streets were dark and quiet.

As she neared the intersection of Burrard and Hastings, she made certain to stay close to the buildings and frequently checked the scans. Her heart rate increased as adrenaline flowed more readily. Still no contact. Her nerves grew increasingly on edge. Something was definitely wrong.

She stopped suddenly when a stray sound of clothing or a shoe being dragged over the sidewalk registered in her helmet sensors.

Pressing her back against a wall made of glass, she drew in a breath and held it when a figure appeared suddenly from a doorway fifty yards ahead. The way the thing moved, a lumbering, stiff-legged gait, she knew it was a zom. One shot in the forehead with her nine-millimeter and the thing would be down. While she might feel a measure of pity for the poor bastard who used to be human, her orders were to avoid contact with the zoms, find the source of the outbreak, and eliminate it.

The stealth suit made her invisible, but zoms were capable of detecting the scent of the living. There was something about the warm blood flowing in human veins that attracted them.

One hour, thirty-five minutes.

Jesse moved backward slowly while keeping her eyes on the zom. It was a male animal. The pale face was half torn away, leaving a blackened gash from the hairline to the jaw exposing the rotting flesh beneath. One eye socket was empty and the clothes were nearly gone from the bone-white, almost translucent flesh.

Around the mouth were traces of dried blood, which meant the thing had eaten not too long ago. What it had dined on wasn't apparent, though Jesse hoped it wasn't human.

As unlikely as that was, the zoms had been swarming the guard posts at the perimeter of the security corridor over the last few months and may have made a meal of one of the guards. The news net was reluctant to share any information about the corridor. Bad news created unrest, and the government didn't need any more headaches.

It was, in fact, the sudden increase in attacks after more than a year of relative quiet in the zone that created the need for a recon probe in the first place. It would have been unlikely she'd have ever gotten a shot at searching for the source of the zombie infections without those attacks. The irony hadn't been lost on her when she presented her argument to command authority.

She was shocked when approval came down from on high so quickly. Two days had to be some kind of record for bureaucratic channels.

The zom had turned and was shuffling in her direction. She wondered if she'd been detected. The thing was alone and since the undead can't talk, she doubted other creatures would be coming after her.

Ducking into the lobby of a building, she drew her gun and waited. *I really don't have time for this*, she thought. According to the grid map on her display screen, her only options were to let the zom go by her or backtrack and go around. This meant there would be no way to get to the street below Hastings without doubling back. And since time was growing short, she'd hide in here and wait for the zom to pass.

After ten minutes had elapsed, the zom reappeared, shuffling along the cracked sidewalk outside the window. Jesse took a step deeper into the darkness and held her breath. The thing had taken a few more steps when it suddenly stopped and slowly turned to face the window.

Raising its arms in front of it, the zom slammed into the window, creating a jagged crack that ran vertically from the base to the top edge of the window. The creature took two steps backward, then again lurched forward and slammed hard into the window, causing the window to finally shatter. Shards of razor-like glass rained down all around the thing, causing deep gashes in its flesh as it lurched through the new opening.

Since the zom was already dead, no blood flowed from the new wounds; instead, a trickle of black sludge oozed from the cuts.

Jesse held up her gun and sighted down the barrel. The silencer muffled the shot as she fired once, creating a perfectly round hole in the center of the zom's forehead. Brains and more sludge erupted out the back of its head and it fell on its back, then lay still.

Stepping closer, careful to avoid contact with the sludge, she studied the creature. When it had been alive, the poor bastard appeared to have been no more than eighteen years old. She'd done him a favor by killing the thing that had taken over his body. Stepping yet closer to the unmoving creature, she peered closely at the head, then her eyes traveled over the river of exploded brains spread across the floor. A sensor in the interface on her arm buzzed softly in her earpiece. The sensor had detected something strange.

The sensor had detected a technological device made of gold and silver and high tech plastics somewhere on the zom. She studied the screen as the sensors further dissected the incoming data and presented her a schematic of the device on the screen.

143

Her eyes widened when she recognized the configuration. An artificial intelligence computer chip had been implanted in the thing. Who would implant such sophisticated technology in a zombie? Why, and for what purpose?

Holstering her gun, Jesse hurried out through the now empty windowsill and made her way along Hastings Street. Burrard was close, no more than fifty yards now.

Odd, she thought. *That zom hadn't been constructed from a patchwork of bodies. It's a single human corpse. How could Intel be so wrong?* A sense of unease rose from deep in her gut. More was happening here than she'd been told.

Following her mission protocols, she could abandon the mission, but her own agenda took priority over those protocols. It was the real reason she'd pushed for this recon and why she'd joined Special Ops. Only a Special Ops agent had the latitude to make adjustments to their orders if the circumstances warranted it. As far as she was concerned, this new information was worth pursuing.

Of course, she would have decided to continue regardless. Her father and brother had been trapped in the infected zone when, after weeks of fighting, the army cordoned off the city center. Upward of fifty thousand people had been sacrificed on the altar of the common good. Though she suspected they were dead, or undead, she wouldn't rest until she knew for sure what had happened to her brother and father.

Jesse suspected the AI chip in the zom she'd destroyed allowed the creature to detect her and that it had relayed her presence to someone. She had just knocked on the back door and a reception committee would no doubt meet her. The odds of her surviving the mission had just dropped to near zero. But however meager her chances, she had to try.

The scar surrounding the implant in her own chest ached, reminding her time was running out.

One hour, twenty-five minutes remained.

She had to tell command about the AI chip. "Dragon to Gargoyle. Over." Static. Then a faint, broken transmission came over her earpiece. "This is Gargoyle... again... –ver."

"Dragon to Gargoyle. Signal quality is poor." Her lips pursed. She had to warn them. "The zoms have an AI chip implanted in them. Do you copy?" More static.

She strained her hearing. Finally a faint voice cut through the hiss. She thought it might be an acknowledgement but couldn't be sure. The hiss became steady so she terminated the link.

Looking up into the moonless sky, she wondered what had happened to the drone. Even the stars were missing, though they hadn't been seen in the night sky for at least a century given the dirty air. She'd taken extra blood oxygen tablets prior to the mission to counteract any possible effects if the suit's filters failed.

Her brow creased. With the loss of communications, her orders were to head immediately to the extraction point, but she had to see this mission through to the end. For her, the mission had always been a one-way trip anyway.

Jesse hoped her stealth suit would allow her to get past any more zoms she might encounter. Of course, if every zom had an AI implant, then she had no chance. She was betting only a few of the things had the implant. *Hell of a thing to bet your life on*, she thought. *But then, I chose the life of a Special Ops agent, didn't I?*

At the intersection she brought up the street grid on the display screen again. The two convention centers were located a block and a half north of her current position.

Dragon Rising

Lying flat on her belly and hidden behind a knee-high marble wall, she crawled to the corner and peeked around the cool stone. The buildings along Burrard Street leading to the convention centers were mostly towers of glass and steel; a hotel sign ran up the side of one. On one side of the street stood an art deco building of tan sandstone. It bristled with gargoyle figures up its length until the structure disappeared in the gloom high overhead.

Focusing her attention farther along Burrard Street with the aid of her night vision equipment, she spotted one of the convention centers. Shadowy, lurching human shapes shambled near the entrance.

The figures didn't generate a heat signature so they had to be zoms. Guards, perhaps? If these things were meant to stop anyone trying to enter, then it was likely at least one had an AI chip like the one she'd already put down.

Studying the zoms using the zoom feature on her ocular implants, she focused on each one in turn. She cursed the fact she was too far away for the sensors to detect the chip. Checking them one by one was taking time, time she didn't have. She wondered if there was a way to tell which one had the AI chip without getting closer.

Her heart rate increased when she noticed one of the zoms standing three steps up near the glass entrance doors. Her eyes narrowed. The things weren't going to stop her. This one seemed to be in charge. The thing had a deep gash across one cheek, and its clothing appeared to be in better condition than the others. Other than the wound on the cheek, the creature was in much better shape than the average zombie. She decided it had to be the one with the AI chip.

146

After counting to three, she held her breath, then leapt to her feet and began to run as fast as she could toward the convention center. Alternating between releasing, then holding her breath, she ran, her heart pounding in her chest. The horizontal stitches around the implant sent waves of needle-like pain shooting across her abdomen, reminding her that failure had serious consequences not only for her but also for the future of the human race.

If the zoms caught her, she'd put the barrel of her gun in her mouth and pull the trigger. No way was she going to become one of those things. No way.

The slap of her boots on the wet pavement echoed off the surrounding buildings. Good thing zoms weren't good at detecting sound.

Her arms pumped as she ran, her gun gripped tightly in her right hand, a finger on the trigger. Glancing briefing to her left, she saw the other convention center come into view. Attached to side of the block-long building was an open breezeway where cruise ships used to come along side. There weren't any zoms near the second convention center so she knew the one she was running toward was the target. At least something was going right.

The zoms in front of the building entrance didn't seem to take any notice of her as she approached. They continued to shuffle and shamble about, seemingly unfocused. The creatures were a nightmare collection of jagged wounds, rotting flesh, and missing appendages and eyes. Their clothing hung in rags off their disintegrating bodies. The smell of rotting flesh leaked through her over-taxed suit filters and was so strong now she could taste it. It soured her stomach. *Crap, these things stink.*

She nimbly dodged the creatures and danced around them, making her way up the black marble steps.

She had nearly reached the glass doors when the zoms' behavior suddenly changed. The zom she suspected contained the AI chip appeared behind her and grabbed her shoulders with both hands and pulled her off her feet. She landed hard on her back. The other zoms now moved up the stairs toward her. She stared wide-eyed over her head, watching them. How had they known to come to the other zom's aid? She was about to be swarmed. No way was she going to be one of them.

Raising her pistol to her temple, she closed her eyes and murmured, "Sorry, Daddy." Squeezing the trigger gradually tighter and tighter, she waited for the inevitable when a sudden sharp pain sent her into a dark abyss.

***

Jesse woke in pitch darkness feeling light-headed. Her mouth was dry and tasted of copper. Her arms ached. When she tried to move, she realized her wrists were tied at her sides. The skin of her wrists felt raw and sore as if she'd been struggling against her bonds.

Her mind raced with possibilities. She might have been rescued, but had she been bitten by a zom? If so, she'd turn soon and become one of them. Her mind was fuzzy. How long was the incubation period again? Shaking her head made sharp pain shoot across her forehead and her scalp. The hair on the back of her head felt damp. Recalling the zombies coming at her, she remembered the smell of them, the pale dead flesh, the rotting, oozing wounds. She shivered. Undead monsters.

She paused.

Someone hit me. Who? She must have blacked out. Now she was here. *But where is here?*

Her heart was pounding in her ears, her harsh breathing was the only sound she could hear. Struggling, she realized she was tied to something flat and hard, like a board. *Where am I?* she thought.

The implant! Ignoring the pain, she strained her neck and willed her eyes to pierce the all-enveloping darkness. Was her AI helmet still working? Her spirits sank as she realized she wasn't wearing it anymore. How long had she been unconscious? Her heart rate increased and her upper lip was damp with sour perspiration. She didn't fear death, but she had to know what had happened to her father and brother before she died.

"Hello?" Her voice echoed, then slowly faded. Wherever she was, it was a large space.

Suddenly subdued lights high in the ceiling came on, adding a soft glow to the room and allowing her to see her surroundings. Swiveling her head, a sense of unease arose in her. As she suspected, the room was large; she estimated fifty-feet square. Along one wall stood upright glass booths containing nude male and female bodies. They looked perfect: athletic and youthful, unmarred by any blemish or wound. Blondes, redheads, brunettes of every shade. Even their skin color was normal; it looked as if blood still flowed in the bodies. Yet they weren't breathing, at least not that she could tell.

Were these the stitched-together zombies Intel had warned her about? If they were, then humanity was in serious trouble. These things could pass for fully human. *They could infiltrate us, then destroy humanity from within.* How was any of this possible and who was behind these creatures?

"You're right to be worried," said a very familiar voice. Shifting her head to her right, she caught her breath when she saw who had spoken. The voice belonged to her father. Her heart sang.

He was alive, but his hazel eyes had an unfamiliar, unsettling look in them.

Her stomach knotted with excitement. "Father! You're alive!"

Stepping closer, her father stopped and one corner of his wide mouth curled up slightly. "Hello, Jesse. It's good to see you."

"Are you here to rescue me?" she asked.

Her father chuckled grimly. He stuffed his hands in the pockets of his gray lab coat. "No. I'm afraid not, my dear." He moved to stand beside what she now saw was a surgical bed she was strapped to. "You and I are on opposite sides of this war. Unless you would like to join Marcus and me."

Jesse's eyes narrowed. What was her father talking about? What war? "Join you?"

Her father sighed. "You and I have disagreed on many things. When you joined Special Ops, I knew I'd lost you forever. But now you can leave all that behind and join us."

He turned and walked to stand before one of the glass tubes containing a heavily muscled, dusky-skinned man. Her father stood with his arms now crossed over his chest, studying the unmoving figure.

"We're building an army to bring order back to the world. Ever since the infection created the zombies, I've been in search of a cure. I haven't discovered one exactly, but I did discover a way to control the infected. That's when it occurred to me humanity needed a strong leader to take charge in these difficult times. They need a ruler to lead them. After the infection the rest of humanity, I will raise them all. Then I will build a paradise that I and I alone control."

He walked back to her and laid a hand on her left arm. "The zombies I raised here AI implants I devised control them. They do my bidding.

150

Your brother was infected and he was my first success. He's waiting outside to greet you, but only if you agree to join us."

Jesse realized her father was insane. The man she knew was gone, replaced by a power-mad despot. He might not be an undead, but he might as well be since he was dead inside.

"Where's my helmet?" she asked.

Her father's mouth formed a grim line. He went to a table near a large refrigeration unit with glass doors that contained glass bottles of liquids with labels she was too far away to read. He returned, holding her helmet. The helmet was made from a cloth-like material and once fitted to the wearer looked like a balaclava. "You mean this toy?"

She nodded. "Will you unroll one side so I see the inside?"

He shrugged and rolled the edge of the helmet back so she could see the data display. The helmet was attuned to her brain waves so only she could read the data. Her heart froze. Ten minutes remained.

"Father, what you're doing is wrong. You know it's wrong. You're playing God."

Her father laughed gruffly, then his eyes narrowed and his brow wrinkled. "The world is in chaos and I mean to save it."

Jesse shook her head. "No. I can't join you. I'd rather die."

Her father grunted, then tossed the helmet on her chest. It landed with the unfurled edge facing her so she could still see the data. The countdown was now at nine minutes, thirty seconds.

In less than ten minutes the mini nuke implanted in her chest would explode, then everything within a ten block radius would be vaporized by a blast of superheated air. She'd be dead, but the mad dream of her father would disappear with the creatures he'd built.

"I'll be back, my dear, sweet Jesse," said her father, his tone edged with sadness.

Dragon Rising

"What are you going to do?" she asked.

He shook his head. "Since you refuse to join me, you will not be reunited with your brother, and I will inject you with the infection. I'll implant an AI chip in your brain so you can join my army. Your skills as a special operations agent will be very useful." Her father turned away and walked to the refrigeration unit. He opened the door and selected a syringe still in its sealed packet.

While he was distracted, Jesse sensed this was her chance. She could give the abort code, or send the code that would activate the nuke early. Not that ten minutes made much difference, but she didn't want to die infected by the zombie virus.

"Gargoyle, this is Dragon, over," she whispered. Stealing a quick glance toward the refrigerator, she saw her father hadn't heard her. Of course she didn't know for certain if her transmission would get through, but she had to try.

She swallowed hard, then she spoke the code words. "Dragon rising." Immediately her chest became warm. Her lips curled in a small smile. Her message had gotten through. *Rest in pea...*

Her consciousness disappeared in a blinding white inferno of superheated air.

Mission complete.

Another Amanda Dark paranormal story, this time told from the point of view of Amanda's spectral client. A story where personal stakes take a horrifying twist.

A Father's Daughter
An Amanda Dark paranormal mystery

R. G. Hart

SAFFRON SHIFTED HER BOTTOM ON THE HARD PINE CHAIr, where she sat studying the unadorned steel-gray walls and floor of the ten-by-ten-foot room surrounding the burnished steel desk in the center of the otherwise bare room. Looking down at herself, she discovered she was dressed in black slacks, flats, and a white cotton long-sleeved shirt. The clothes reminded her of the K-Mart housewives she silently mocked when she made trips to the mall to visit the high-end shops for new shoes and the latest fashions. She had closets reserved just for her shoes. She had never worn such frumpy clothes in her life.

Seated across from her in a brown, well-worn leather chair was a pale-faced, severe-looking woman with mint green eyes, her angular features focused on the pages of a large, clothbound book, open on the desk in front of her.

Saffron had no sense of how long she'd been here or how she'd gotten here. But she did have a vague sense of unease, deep in her belly, that had formed a knot reminiscent of hunger.

Dragon Rising

Yet she wasn't hungry, at least not exactly, as she thought of hunger. In the recesses of her mind, memoires bubbled of the taste of champagne and cherries and coffee, but she had no compulsion or need for them. Something had changed. But what?

Saffron's auburn eyes finally landed on the woman across from her, who smelled of peppermints and chamomile tea like her grandmother, who had died when she and her twin sister, Sadie, were fifteen years old. Their father had taken them with him to retrieve her grandmother's clothes for the funeral. She recalled seeing the hairbrush lying faceup on her grandmother's antique mirrored dresser, the battleship-gray wisps of hair still clinging to the stiff, black horsehair bristles as if trapped for eternity as the only remaining evidence of the woman who gave her chocolate candies at Christmas and sent crisp, new dollar bills for her and her sister in a birthday card each year.

A twinge of regret for the unkindness toward her elderly grandmother invaded her thoughts briefly, then retreated immediately. As long as she could recall, her grandmother had been trapped in a frail body twisted by painful arthritis. Saffron had been young and stupid then, a horribly self-absorbed teenager who failed to appreciate her elders.

Her deepest regret was reserved for her father, whose angry eyes bore into her when, at her grandmother's funeral, she and her sister had giggled at some inane private joke between them.

Mercifully he never spoke to her about the incident, but she knew they had disappointed him. Her beloved father was the only man she had ever looked to for wisdom and guidance. Most of the men she dated were spoiled pretty-boys with more money than brains. They definitely weren't the type of men she would ever marry or turn to for advice.

She had always wanted to apologize to her father for her behavior, but had never had the courage to bring up the subject with him. Since that day, she'd considered their relationship irrecoverably damaged.

Looking around the bare room, she somehow sensed that her opportunity to tell her father how she felt had passed.

"Miss Smythe?" said the woman, startling her from her moment of retrospection. The woman's voice had a deep timber and an edge of disapproval. Hanging from her neck by a thin chain was a pair of horn-rimmed glasses. She was wearing a dowdy dress of navy-blue roses over a pale beige background. A button at the neck secured the collar. Her dark hair was shot through with gray streaks and was tied into a bun atop her narrow head.

"Yes. Saffron Smythe, actually."

One pepper-colored eyebrow arched on her pale forehead as she regarded Saffron, obviously unimpressed. "Yes," she said, "Saffron, of course." The woman interlaced her long, tapered fingers on top of the pages of the open book, then leaned slightly forward, her elbows resting on the book. Her dispassionate gaze made Saffron uncomfortable. "According to our records, you are here slightly earlier than expected."

"Ummmm, that's the thing, Ms...." Saffron looked at the woman questioningly.

"Ruth. You may call me Ruth." A slight hitch in Ruth's tone suggested Saffron was to continue. She had a small, humorless smile on her lips.

Saffron nodded. "I'm not sure where I am, exactly."

The woman nodded, unlaced her fingers, and eased back in her chair, her expression sending Saffron signals that she had heard this question many times.

"Of course. Many who arrive here have no idea their existence on Earth is at an end."

Saffron froze and her jaw dropped. She shivered as if she was suddenly chilled, except the room's temperature was nearly perfect. "Do you mean I'm dead?"

A sardonic smile spread across Ruth's features. "Yes. But don't be concerned. You're in the best of hands. I'll soon have your next assignment ready."

"But I can't be dead," Saffron whispered. "I'm too young. And I'm too rich."

Ruth grinned. "I hear that a lot; more often than you might think, actually."

Anger bubbled up from Saffron's stomach. She tasted sour bile at the back of her throat. *How can I be dead and still taste bile?* She sucked in a breath, then exhaled. *I seem to be breathing.* She pinched the skin of her right arm between thumb and forefinger as hard as she could, and winced at the sudden rush of pain. *Son of a bi*—She spat her next words between gritted teeth. "Lady, I don't know who you are, but I'm the daughter of a very powerful man, so I suggest you let me go immediately."

"Oh, but Saffron, no one is holding you here, I assure you. This is a way station. My job is to prepare you for your final destination."

Saffron's anger subsided and she eyed the woman. "Final destination?" She had a bad feeling about Ruth's answer. She knew somehow she wouldn't like it.

A sardonic grin came over Ruth's pale features and her eyes narrowed. "Yes," Ruth said simply, offering no further explanation.

Saffron tried to recall where she had been and what she had been doing before realizing she was in this windowless room across a desk from this woman who reeked of peppermints.

156

No matter how she tried, it was as if her mind was in a fog.

"It's OK, Saffron. It's unlikely you'll be able to recall anything from the time before you died except for flashes of stray thoughts that may seem like dreams. But don't be concerned. This is often taxing on new arrivals at first, but with time, you will understand. Most new arrivals find that when they are allowed into the hall of memories, they begin to comprehend what they had been in life and what they are now." Ruth spoke as if these cryptic words made perfect sense; however, Saffron remained thoroughly confused.

This lady is nutso. "OK, I get it, I'm dead and this is heaven... but how did I die?" Saffron froze when an image suddenly formed of herself lying in a bathtub, buried in an ocean of white foam. She was somehow hovering over herself, looking down at her naked form through the dissipating bubbles, lying on her back under the water in the marble tub. Her body was limp, unmoving, her eyes closed. Saffron realized the her in the bathtub wasn't breathing and the lips were pale, the skin on the face a sickly gray pallor. A half empty crystal champagne flute sat on the edge of the tub. The bubbles in the wine having long ago dispersed meant the flute had sat untouched for too long and gone flat.

It dawned on her she had died while having a bubble bath.

She loved bubble baths, the water lapping against her skin like a silk blanket, the warm steam rising from the white jasmine-scented bubbles. Surely she wasn't meant to die in a bath? Saffron licked her lips. *I loved the taste of champagne on my tongue.*

Ruth laughed lightly, causing the corners of her eyes to crinkle. "No, this isn't heaven. As I said before, this is a way station where you will receive your next assignment."

Saffron studied the woman's placid features, then her eyes dropped to look at the book.

"What's in the book?" she asked.

"This is a record of each person's date of death. My job is to fill in the column listing each arrival's final destination—once I'm told, of course."

Saffron's eyes narrowed. "Told? Told by whom?"

Suddenly a telephone began to emit a muffled ring. Ruth smiled and reached down to open a drawer in the desk beside her. She withdrew a telephone as black as licorice, with a heavy black wire trailing off the back of the unit and a dial face on the front, covering a white background depicting large numbers and small block letters under each opening in the dial. There was a receiver in a cradle on the top, attached the main body by a wire. As Ruth set it on the desk with a soft thump, it rang again, only louder this time since the drawer didn't muffle it.

Saffron had never seen a telephone like it. Where was Ruth's cell phone?

Ruth picked up the receiver and held it to her ear. "Yes?" She listened intently to whomever had called, her expression changing from pleased, to concerned, to puzzled. Finally she said good-bye and hung up. Her eyes reflected her astonishment.

She sighed before she spoke. "This happens so rarely I am surprised every time it does." Ruth paused, adding to Saffron's discomfort. Finally she continued. "I'm advised you are to be sent back to Earth."

She paused again to look into Saffron's eyes since they must have revealed her excitement.

I'm going home.

"I'm sorry, I'm not being clear. Your spirit will be sent to Earth, but your interaction with living beings will be quite limited." Ruth cleared her throat, Saffron sensing the woman's hesitation.

"It appears you have indeed arrived earlier than expected because you were murdered."

Oh, shit. I'm in trouble. I need Amanda Dark.

***

Saffron had no sense of movement but she suddenly materialized in Phillip Swann's office, one of many in the law offices of Smythe, Wellington, Goldberg, and Thompson. Her senses were immediately assaulted by the scent of wood polish, which wasn't surprising as the Boston law firm had never removed the original teak paneling, installed when the prestigious firm opened in 1902. Such expensive wood required constant care to maintain its gleaming, pristine appearance, but the partners agreed it added to the firm's elegant image. The firm had represented Boston's social elite worldwide for over a hundred years. Of course, she knew this because her great-great-great-grandfather had been the founder and an original partner of the firm. Her father still represented the family name on the masthead.

Before the way station disappeared as if in a fog, Ruth explained Saffron had been granted one visit outside the place she was to haunt until the matter of her murder was settled. By settled, of course, Ruth meant the murder was solved and the killer brought to justice. Only then would Saffron return to the way station to be assigned her final destination.

She would be able to interact with one living person and be able to experience sensory details of the environment around her since this might help trigger memories essential to solving the crime. Ruth ended by warning her it might take some time, so she must be patient.

Dragon Rising

As if looking through a veil of mist, Saffron saw Phillip Swann come into focus. He was seated in a black leather executive chair behind a massive, fifty-year-old teak desk, examining documents one by one from a thick file. The wood of the desk was stained dark and polished to a gleaming shine under the light of the crystal chandelier in the ten-foot-high ceiling overhead. A silver executive telephone was to Phillip's right and a large, flat computer screen was to his left. Behind his desk and running the length of the long office wall were built-in bookcases containing volumes of law books. One wall was a floor-to-ceiling picture window overlooking the bustling city streets far below. The glass was tinted so it wasn't too bright in the offices, even on the sunniest of days.

But Saffron's attention was drawn to Amanda Dark, who was seated in a horseshoe-shaped leather chair, watching Phillip from the other side of his massive desk. Amanda was a short woman, just over five feet in height; of medium build, not buxom and not thin; with mouse-brown hair cut to brush her shoulders. Her pleasant features, wide-set, curious hazel eyes, and smallish nose meant she couldn't be described as beautiful, but she wasn't ugly, either. Right now Amanda's eyes gazed at Phillip with a look in them Saffron knew well. The woman loved the firm's associate more than she was willing to admit.

With his jet-black, curly hair cut military short, his square jaw, and dimples in both cheeks when he smiled, Saffron well understood Phillip's appeal. His narrow waist and lightly muscled arms under his tailored suits and shirts told her he took care of his appearance, but then, any lawyer whose goal was to become a partner needed every weapon in his arsenal to get there. Phillip Swann was bright, personable, and good looking, so he'd surely make partner someday.

Saffron had met Phillip and Amanda at one of her father's mixers held in the office a couple of times a year. Normally she avoided such stuffy affairs, preferring to hit the many clubs and bars around Boston with peers her own age; but for some reason, that day she attended the party where she met the young, handsome associate and his unlikely wannabe girlfriend.

Amanda claimed to be a paranormal detective. She hadn't explained what the job entailed, but Saffron soon learned that the plain-speaking woman had helped Phillip on a number of difficult estate cases resulting in very grateful and very wealthy clients who paid considerable sums to the firm. Once, after a few too many drinks, her father told her Amanda Dark was a ghost whisperer and that she could speak to the spirits of the dead. Saffron thought this nonsense; she didn't believe in ghosts.

But when Ruth asked who she would like to see on Earth, Saffron immediately asked for Amanda Dark. Even if she were a fake, she had helped some big cases for the firm so she had to have some talent for dealing with the paranormal—or she was the most successful grifter in history. Seeing Amanda's K-Mart wardrobe of gray cotton slacks, white, no-name-brand runners, and sleeveless, mint-green rayon top didn't scream flourishing con artist. Saffron doubted the latter was true.

Suddenly Saffron froze as Amanda visibly stiffened. She was looking right at her, her eyes growing wide—not with fear but with surprise. *She sees me now.*

"Uh, Phil, we have a visitor," Amanda said in a low voice.

"Ummm," said Phillip, his attention focused on a document he was reading from the file folder. "Tell them I'm busy."

"It's not that kind of visitor," explained Amanda, her voice louder now.

Phillip stopped reading as his brow wrinkled and he looked up at Amanda. "A ghost?" he asked as if it were an everyday occurrence. In fact, Saffron could swear his expression was one of annoyance. "In my office?" He shook his head. "No way. We've never had a ghost in my office. You must be mistaken."

Amanda shook her head, her eyes still locked on Saffron, who stood still with a tight grin on her lips. "In fact, I think it's Robert Smythe's daughter."

Phillip grunted. "Really? Which one?" He scanned the room. "I don't see anyone."

Amanda turned her head to scowl at him as if he were a small child. "Really, Phil, do we have to go through this again?"

Phillip's shoulders relaxed and he grinned, the dimples in his cheeks deepening. "I'm kidding, Amanda. Surely by now you know when I'm joking?"

The tension in Amanda's body eased and she chuckled. "Sorry, Phil, but you know how I am about my work."

"Amanda," interrupted Saffron, "have you two finished your mating dance yet? I have a big problem I need your help with."

Amanda shifted her attention to Saffron. "Sorry, Ms. Smythe, Phil and I are so used to ghosts and we too often verbally spar in front of them." Her hazel eyes flitted to a grinning Phillip Swann, who eased back in his chair while maintaining his silence, then back to her. "What can I do for you?"

These two seemed to be laughing at her. *I've been murdered, for God's sake.*

A knot of anger formed in her stomach. Old habits from her impetuous, over-privileged youth were going to be tougher to break than she thought.

She could not deny it; in life she had been a rich, spoiled brat, but now that she was dead, she had vowed to be better in the afterlife.

She managed to push the anger away before she spoke. "Please call me Saffron. Ms. Smythe was my late mother, God rest her soul." She paused as the humor faded from Amanda's eyes. Saffron then blurted, "I've been murdered. I desperately need your help to catch the killer."

***

Saffron stood on the cold marble floor of the expansive foyer of Smythe Hall, Amanda beside her. The sweeping circular staircase curled up and into the distance to the upper floors of the ten-bedroom, ten-bathroom mansion. The floor-to-ceiling crushed-red-velvet drapes over the tall windows bordering the cool foyer were drawn shut, requiring the large crystal chandelier hanging twenty-five feet above their heads to be illuminated, even though it was early afternoon on a summer day. The musty air spoke of age and neglect. Saffron realized something had happened in her family home—something bad.

Amanda coughed to clear her throat. "Phil said your father agreed to meet me...I mean us."

"You didn't tell him about me, did you?"

Amanda shook her head. "If I did, do you think he would agree to see me?"

Saffron sighed. Of course Amanda was correct. If she told him she had spoken to his dead daughter, he'd have dismissed her as a kook after his money. Her father was a practical man if nothing else.

"I have a question."

Amanda looked at her with a curious expression.

Saffron continued, "How can I be dead so long but only now become..." Her words trailed off. She couldn't say the word ghost, it sounded ridiculous.

How long ago did I die? For the first time, it occurred to her to wonder how long she'd been dead.

"When did I die?"

Amanda's brow wrinkled. "Space and time are very different in the afterlife. Time isn't linear—"

She was about to explain more when somewhere overhead a generator suddenly whirred to life in the silent, dusty air that stank of stale coffee and burnt toast, interrupting them. Amanda's eyes suggested that later might be a better time to talk.

Reluctantly Saffron agreed. She had a sense time was short, even though in reality she had more time now than she'd ever had in life.

Saffron saw a slit of light coming from the bottom of a closet door on the left side of the foyer that, as she recalled, contained her mother's and father's long evening coats.

The slit of light grew brighter as a rumbling sound and the whine of the generator increased in intensity. Finally there was a deep thud and the door of the closet slid aside to reveal a wizened man with white hair in a wheelchair. His gray eyes studied Amanda, his pale brow wrinkled by curiosity.

Saffron sucked in a breath as the man's long fingers worked a control stick on the right armrest of the wheelchair and it rolled out of the closet, now obviously converted to an elevator, onto the marble floor. Tears blurred her vision as she realized the man was her father.

The once vital, healthy man who drank protein shakes for breakfast, ran in marathons, and worked out at the firm's gym three times a week had been replaced by these fossil-like remains.

Amanda's features were lit by a smile as she stepped forward to greet her father in the wheelchair. He appeared worn and tired, his once alert, steady gaze dull and lifeless as if he'd lost hope. His features were gaunt, his cheeks sunken, his skin had a gray pallor.

Upon fully seeing his appearance, Saffron's heart ached for her father as her eyes welled with tears. Ruth promised she'd experience everything she saw, heard, and smelled—complete with the accompanying emotional reactions—as if she were still alive. But she'd be unable to offer comfort to those who needed it or speak with anyone other than Amanda.

If I'd only known my father needed me so badly, I would have asked to speak with him instead of Amanda. She may not have been able to solve her murder, but her father needed her and that was more important right now.

Amanda stuck out one hand, which her father ignored, preferring to keep his hands folded in his lap. He was dressed in a navy-blue tracksuit, his feet covered by slippers that were almost worn through with use. The front of the zippered jacket was covered in soup stains. "Mr. Smythe, it's a pleasure to see you again, sir. How long has it been? Ten years?"

His eyes narrowed. "Do I know you?" he asked, his voice raspy and dry.

Amanda dropped her hand to her side, her smile still bright and inviting. "I'm Amanda Dark. Phillip Swann's friend."

His brow creased in thought for several seconds until he nodded. "Yes, the ghost person. You talk to the dead."

"Yes, sir, I am blessed, or some would say cursed, with that particular gift."

The old man eyed her with one gray eyebrow arched. "My daughter died eight years ago. Are you communicating with her ghost now, is that why you're here?" He snorted bitterly. "And I suppose you want money."

Amanda shook her head. "No, sir, Phillip works for you at the firm and your daughter approached us asking for our help. We won't be billing anything for my services."

Robert Swann shook his head. "She died in a car accident. Why would she want to talk to me now, after all this time?"

Car accident? thought Saffron. "Amanda, who died in a car accident? I drowned in a bathtub. I remember it."

Amanda nodded to Saffron. "Sir, I thought your daughter drowned."

Robert laughed derisively, his humor tainted with bitterness. "No, no, that's Saffron. That lazy, ungrateful drunk drowned herself after partying all night with her so-called friends. She spent my money recklessly and selfishly. She deserved to die." He paused and hung his head.

"My precious Sadie, she died in the car wreck not a mile from the estate. Her death ended my life's work." A tear escaped his right eye, running down his cheek until it fell off the edge of his bony chin to splash on the foyer floor.

Saffron couldn't believe what she was hearing. If she had been murdered, then either her father had done it or her beloved twin sister had done the deed. She suspected she'd been drugged, then passed out in the bathtub and drowned. An engineered accident covered up by a powerful law firm with friends in high places, including the police department.

"Amanda," Saffron whispered. "Don't go any further. I don't want to know."

Amanda looked at her with wide eyes. "But it means you won't be able to go to your final destination, ever."

"Are you crazy, woman?" asked Robert, his eyes wild and his cheeks flushed by a surge of anger. "Who are you talking to?"

Amanda turned to face Robert in his wheelchair. "Your daughter, Saffron, is here with me," she said, glaring at him. "And right now, I must explain a few things to her; then you and I must talk. Sir," she added firmly, her hazel eyes now hard, the smile but a memory.

Robert sagged in his chair, his hands fidgeting erratically in his lap, his face twisted by a scowl.

Amanda faced Saffron. "I checked your file at Phillip's office before I came here." She paused and Saffron could see the mix of emotions on her wholesome features. The paranormal detective took in a deep breath to steady herself and then continued. "Yes, you died in the bath. Drowned, as you say. The police investigated after the coroner determined you had an overdose of sleeping pills in your blood stream.

"The investigation resulted in a ruling of accidental overdose, which led to your drowning. Then there was a notation found in your diary—"

"Sadie wrote the suicide note in Saffron's diary," Robert suddenly blurted, his words angry. "I provided the overdose of pills. I killed my own daughter." He steered the wheelchair across the marble floor, right at Amanda, who stepped aside as he stopped. He stuck out a bony index finger at her. "And I'd do it again. Sadie deserved a chance to run the firm. She was a lawyer, but their late mother, who controlled the real family money, included a clause in her will that required the firm be sold after my death and the proceeds divided equally between the twins.

"Sadie would have saved my firm from extinction. Saffron was a party girl who would have destroyed the firm I built. All she cared about was satisfying her own selfish pleasures. If anything happened to Sadie after I died, Saffron would have assumed control of the firm." He sagged in his chair and his voice dropped to a hoarse whisper. "I couldn't let that happen.

"Sadie would have kept up the family tradition. Saffron deserved to die so her sister could inherit the business." He paused when his voice cracked. Clearing his throat, Robert shook his head. "It seemed to make sense then...now that my own days are numbered, I'm not so sure."

His watery gaze shifted to Amanda. "I realize now I was wrong. Tell Saffron I'm sorry. I made a mistake." He began to sob, and Saffron sensed his terrible pain and regret.

Amanda looked again at Saffron. "Well, what do you want to do?"

Saffron thought for a few seconds and then made up her mind. "I'm going to stay at Smythe Hall by my father's side until he dies. I still love him and I forgive him."

"You do know you won't be able to change your mind?"

Saffron nodded.

The doorbell rang, interrupting them. Amanda went to the window and pulled the drape aside. Phillip stood at the door. She waved to him, then turned back to face Robert Smythe, who gazed back at her with red-rimmed eyes.

"Mr. Smythe, I'm going to leave you now. I wish you well, sir, but I still feel your daughter has made a poor decision. If I had my way, and there were sufficient evidence, I would go to the police. But I imagine the extensive cover-up of your crime and the fact it occurred ten years ago make any investigation not worthwhile."

Ignoring Amanda's words, Robert Smythe's eyes reflect his realization that his murdered daughter's spirit was in the room with them. "What did Saffron decide?"

"She's forgiven you and will be staying on as the resident ghost of Smythe Hall." The corners of Amanda's mouth curled up slightly as she shared a knowing look with Saffron. "At least for a while."

Amanda then opened the front door and went outside, closing it with a soft thump behind her.

Saffron gazed at her father in his wheelchair, his pale gray eyes fearful, and wondered how long he would live. She would haunt him until then, hopefully helping him to come to grips with what he had done and the consequences he might suffer when his day at the way station came. She wondered where Ruth would assign him. Probably not the place with the wings.

One thing she knew for certain; she would see Amanda Dark again, when the time was right.

Finally, we leave you with an Amanda Dark tale that starts as a routine case but turns into a nightmare of personal terror for Amanda. She is forced to confront dark family secrets and the resulting emotional fallout.

Moonrise Diner
An Amanda Dark Paranormal Mystery

Russ Crossley

THE CUSHIONS OF PHILLIP SWANN'S BLACK LEATHER EXECUTIVE CHAIR sighed as he sank into it, breaking the silence of the teak wood paneled office. Amanda Dark sat in a horseshoe-shaped chair studying him from the other side of his massive, glass-topped desk. His intense blue eyes were fixed on the letter he'd unfolded seconds ago after extracting it from the yellowing envelope Amanda had handed him when she sat down.

His jet-black, curly hair, cut short as usual, appealed to her more every day they spent together. Her heart beat a little faster each time they met. If only he shared her deeper feelings.

The law offices of Smythe, Wellington, Goldberg & Thompson smelled of wood polish, which wasn't surprising since the Boston law firm had never removed the teak paneling from the walls, installed when the firm first opened in 1902. Such expensive wood required constant care to maintain its gleaming, pristine appearance.

Amanda imagined such attention to detail gave the firm's wealthy clients considerable confidence in the expertise of the firm's seventy-five lawyers. Amanda eyed Phillip's square jaw, dimpled smile, and broad shoulders. Her heart fluttered.

I certainly have confidence in the man I've loved since we met on Hook Island.

Their first meeting had been eventful and dangerous, so it wasn't a stretch to remember those events. Phillip had invited her to Hook Island, hoping she'd use her gift to help the ghost of the notorious pirate, Captain Henry Swann, his ancestor, to cross over to his final destination. Phillip had wanted to free the pirate captain from his wanderings between this world and the next. And he had wanted her to ask his ancestor the location of a map so he could find Captain Swann's buried treasure, reported to be worth a fortune.

Since then, Phillip, as an estate attorney, had teamed up with her, in her role as a paranormal investigator, to help a number of tortured souls to cross over. The jobs had been rewarding and lucrative for them both. Wealthy clients paid considerable sums for their services.

Phillip finished reading the three-page letter and set it carefully on his desk. The document was quite old, dating back to the nineteen fifties. She knew this because it had been in her late father's files.

Amanda had found the envelope in a file folder stuffed with power company bills from the early fifties she'd been about to throw away. She hadn't opened the envelope addressed to her father because the return address was for her Uncle Gib's place in Arizona.

Uncle Gib, her father's older brother, had sexually abused her when she was twelve, so anything he had touched repulsed her. Her first thought was to burn the envelope to a pile of ash to join her uncle, who no doubt burned in hell. But something deep within told her not to destroy this envelope.

These feelings were something more than mere emotions; it was important she listen to the spiritual voices calling to her.

The postmark showed the letter was mailed from Moonrise, Arizona. The date stamp in the postmark intrigued her the most because it was the day her uncle murdered his first wife, Lucy. Or, at least, the day he allegedly stabbed her to death.

Her uncle had been acquitted of the murder but had lived under a cloud of suspicion for the rest of his life. Family legend said Gib remarried, his second wife also named Luci (the only difference being her name ended in an *i* instead of a *y*). Like his first wife, she worked as a waitress for him at the Moonrise Diner. There could have been physical differences as well, but Amanda never met either of them, so she had no idea what they looked like.

As far as she knew, no one in the family had ever met Luci the second, even after Gib died. Frankly, Amanda thought there never was a second wife.

Amanda had searched the on-line newspaper archives after she found the envelope and discovered coverage of Gib's trial. There was no mention in any of the news articles of a letter mailed to her father on the day of Gib's arrest. And there was no mention of her father testifying at her uncle's trial.

Her father had told her he turned his back on his brother after his arrest; they hadn't reconciled until after she was born. Her father never explained how they buried the figurative hatchet to settle their differences.

At the time Uncle Gib abused her, she feared that telling her father would create another split between the two brothers, so she remained silent. Fortunately, the abuse only happened once. Then

Gib left Boston for the last time. When Amanda was thirteen, Gibb ended his own life.

She'd blocked his name from her mind for the past fourteen years until she found the envelope.

Phillip, his eyes on the desk, his head forward, didn't say anything for several minutes. The suspense formed a knot of tension in Amanda's stomach and she grew increasingly restless as Phillip deliberated. She passed the time by shifting her bottom on the leather chair repeatedly as if she were unable to get comfortable. Finally, she couldn't contain herself any further. "Phillip, for goodness' sake, what does it say?"

Phillip looked up from the desk, his eyes free of emotion, to lock eyes with her. One eyebrow arched on his tanned forehead. "Your uncle wasn't who he said he was."

Her heart skipped a beat. *Breathe, girl....*"What do you mean?"

Phillip sat back and sighed. "He claims he was an undercover operative for the Arizona State Police. He says someone killed his wife to send him a message."

"Does he say who?" Now she was extremely interested. This had quickly become a mystery. She loved a mystery.

Phillip gazed at her, a pained expression on his face. "Something about inappropriate advances on a woman." He looked away, avoiding her stare.

Amanda's guts twisted, pushing the acid taste of bile into the back of her throat. She thought she might vomit at any second. She shuddered as the awful memory of her uncle's groping hands swept over her. Memories of the stale liquor on his breath, the smell of salty sweat, and the spent cooking grease leaching from his pores paralyzed her.

"Did he know who killed his wife?" she whispered in a trembling

174

voice. Calling on inner reserves, she pushed through the decades of pain and humiliation.

Phillip shook his head.

Her Uncle Gib was a creepy, lying, sack of...but he was her beloved father's brother, and his wife had apparently been murdered by persons unknown. And who knew now if his death was a suicide? Everything about the letter cast uncertainty on her uncle's life, requiring closer scrutiny. In respect for her dad's love for his brother, she would solve this mystery. Given her history with her uncle, she just didn't want to.

"I'll call the Arizona State Police, then," she decided. "They'll look into the murder." Phillip shook his head again, the difference this time being his eyes drooped at the corners.

A sudden burst of anger welled up from deep within Amanda's belly. *I don't need his pity.*

"Did I say something wrong?" asked Phillip, his eyes wide with concern.

"Why do you ask?"

Phillip's expression relaxed. "Ummm, I know this is a stressful situation, Amanda, and I'm sorry, I truly am." A gentle smile passed over his handsome features.

When she'd brought him the envelope, she'd told him how she didn't like her uncle and that he was estranged from the family, but didn't share the details of the sexual abuse. But her would-be boyfriend was a smart man; he knew something was very wrong even if he didn't know the details. "But the Arizona state cops are unlikely to take any interest in reopening the case. They seemed convinced your uncle committed the crime."

Amanda picked up the glass of water Phillip had poured for her when she first arrived and took a sip of the cool water as the tension in her body eased. "Why not? I'm sure they want to catch the real murderer."

Phillip nodded. "Of course, but the case was likely closed after your uncle's trial because they probably still think he's guilty, or got off on some technicality, or he had a clever lawyer." His mouth formed a sly smile. "They don't much care for the practitioners of my profession. And if you tell them you're a paranormal investigator, they'll laughed us both out of the police station."

Amanda's cheeks grew warm. "What's wrong with my job?"

Phillip arched one eyebrow. "Now, Amanda, I don't mean to offend you. I know from personal experience you have a special gift, but police officers are born skeptics. They'll never take you seriously." He sighed, then lifted his coffee mug to his lips and took a sip. After swallowing he added, "I think the better approach is to search the scene of the crime for ourselves. Maybe we'll find something, or someone, that'll help us uncover the truth. Something the cops overlooked all those years ago."

The anger disappeared as Amanda considered his words. He was right. They both knew the "something or someone" Phillip referred to involved ghosts and the paranormal.

"OK," she said, "the place to start is the town of Moonrise, Arizona. That's where Gib had his diner—his wife, Lucy, died in the diner..." Her brow wrinkled. "And I seem to recall Dad telling me Gib committed suicide in the diner."

Her well-tuned sixth sense for the supernatural told her they would find a horrible truth at the Moonrise Diner, a frightening truth that made her blood run cold.

***

The two lanes of cracked asphalt that were the main street of Moonrise,

Arizona were off the state highway on an old bypass carved from the dry, desolate landscape surrounding the abandoned mining town. According to the GPS navigator, the bypass ended five miles north of the town.

Amanda spent the several-hour drive to Moonrise from the Phoenix airport on her iPad reviewing the transcript of her uncle's trial that Phillip had managed to obtain for her. She was surprised the file even existed anymore, but was pleased it was found in the Arizona State Government Library.

The transcript did yield some interesting facts. In 1972, Uncle Gib testified he and Lucy had a fierce argument the night Lucy was killed, after which he went to a nearby bar to cool off—ending up going on a drinking binge. There were a plethora of names related to the case—small-time gangsters mostly, with colorful names like Pete "Split Nose" Rostovitch, Jimmy "Beer Belly" Lucia, Al "Stinky" Garbone, and Max "Maximum Guts" Schiller.

Uncle Gib claimed one of these gangsters killed his wife, but his reasons for thinking this were absent from the record. The cops or the district attorney obviously didn't believe his allegations, or they didn't want to believe him.

She put her iPad away in her handbag as Phillip stopped their rented Jeep in front of the Moonrise Hotel. Amanda expected to see a hitching post for horses, and cowboys with ten-gallon hats and leather gun belts strapped to their hips standing on the porch.

Instead, a gray-haired man sat in a rocking chair reading a newspaper on the porch to one side of the twin doors of the hotel entrance. The doors had glass windows built into the wood frame, allowing her to see the lobby and the front desk. A gray-haired woman stood behind the desk, her eyes focused on something in front of her.

Phillip shut off the engine, then swung the driver's door open as the rumble of the engine died away and was replaced by the soft whisper of the desert wind.

The oppressive heat struck her in the face as soon as she swung the passenger door open. Her skin immediately became damp with sweat as she stepped into the thick, hot air.

Phillip retrieved their suitcases from the back of the jeep, then joined her walking up the three steps to the wide, gray wood porch, the boards creaking underfoot.

The man in the rocker lowered his newspaper and his coffee-colored eyes narrowed. "Heya, you folks lookin' for a room?" His voice had a scratchy quality like an old phonograph record.

"Yes," said Amanda, with a nice-to-meet-you smile on her lips. "We're in town on vacation."

The man chuckled gruffly, letting the newspaper fall into his lap. "Vacation? In Moonrise? That's a good one, young lady." He arched one white eyebrow. "No one vacations in this town. It's nearly dead. Me and the wife are the last of the few who stayed after the silver mine closed."

"When was that?" asked Phillip.

The old man snorted. "Back in '99. The mining company ran out of money...they left town along with most of the folks 'round here." He peered into the distance, ignoring them. "We had a pretty young school marm, a church, a general store, and even one of them fancy haberdasheries.... those were the days..." He scowled and abruptly raised the newspaper, creating a wall of newsprint between them. "Never been the same since," he muttered.

Amanda shook her head and then caught herself when she

spotted the date at the top of the paper in the old man's hands. November 21, 1910.

That can't be right. Has to be a misprint.

Phillip opened one of the twin glass-and-wood doors and ushered her inside. Once in the hotel lobby, the smell of dust and sand disappeared, replaced by the scent of jasmine; and though the air was warm, it was cooler than outside. The reception desk, made of weathered wood planks, sat to the left of a wide, sweeping staircase, reminiscent of *Gone With the Wind*, which rose from the floral-patterned carpet in the lobby to disappear to the floors above.

A woman behind the desk cast her dispassionate gaze over them. The collar of her old-fashioned, long-sleeved dress covered her long, narrow neck to just under her angular chin. Her hollow, sunken eyes were the color of obsidian and her complexion reminded Amanda of white glue. *Maybe she's ill...*

"Hello," she said in a rasping voice. "May I help you?"

"Yes, ma'am," said Phillip, his tone musical and friendly. Overly friendly, it sounded false to Amanda and probably everyone else. She cringed inside. Regardless, he continued. "We need two rooms, please."

The old woman smirked and flopped open a register, sending a puff of dust into the air.

Amanda waved away the dust, blinking her eyes to clear them. "Two rooms?" she whispered to Phillip. "Why don't we share one? It'd be cheaper."

He turned his head slightly to look at her. "Best to have separate rooms." He grinned. "I might not be able to control myself."

Amanda offered a weak grin. *I only wish.* She immediately scolded herself. *I'm acting like a lovesick schoolgirl; I'm a grown woman.*

"How long have you been here?" Amanda asked the woman.

"All my life, Miss."

"Sorry, I meant how long has the hotel been here?"

"Longer than I have."

Amanda studied the woman, looking for signs she was joking, but she appeared to be serious so Amanda shifted her gaze to look at Phillip. He offered her a humorless smile but didn't say anything.

After Phillip signed the register for them both, the old woman placed two old-fashioned brass keys with yellowing paper tags attached to the ends on the counter. Her eyes dropped to peer at the two names Phillip had recorded in the ledger.

"Mr. Swann, I gave you room 212." Her eyes shifted to Amanda, "Room 312 for you, Miss Dark." The woman's tone was clipped and registered her disapproval of Amanda.

I guess she doesn't like questions.

"I'll carry your bag to your room," offered Phillip.

"No, thank you, Mr. Swann, I carry my own weight." Amanda snatched her room key off the desk and then, after grabbing her bag by the handle, hurried up the curved, carpeted staircase, headed for the rooms on the upper floor.

"I'll meet you here in the lobby in half an hour," Phillip called after her.

"OK." Without looking back, she hurried up the creaking stairs. She hoped they had Wi-Fi. The man and woman running the hotel seemed strangely out of place, though they claimed to have been living in Moonrise all their lives. She needed to conduct some research about the town and its remaining inhabitants.

***

The first thing she noticed upon entering the room was the smell. It reeked of mothballs and cigarette smoke.

There was an old-fashioned gas lamp on an end table next to an antique, burnished brass bed frame containing a too-soft mattress that sagged badly under the weight of her suitcase, which wasn't much since she'd packed light.

She set up her laptop on the cheap pine table under the window overlooking the street in front of the hotel. Moving the matching chair away from the desk, she sat down and flipped the laptop open. After booting it up, she saw there was no Wi-Fi connection.

Disappointed, she next opened the folder with the pictures she'd downloaded of her uncle's diner from the family electronic archive her sister had set up years before, then clicked through them one by one. As she studied the photos, her mouth became dry and a lump of emotion grew in her throat as memories, both good and bad, washed over her.

She stopped clicking the cursor, now hovering over an image of Uncle Gib's diner back in the days he and Lucy owned it, wondering if she'd be able to overcome her fears and dread to go inside. But she knew she had to; it was the only way she'd discover the truth.

A picture of the diner, severely dilapidated—it had been abandoned after her uncle's death—replaced the image of the pristine diner on her screen.

Somehow Amanda knew they'd discover the ghost of Lucy Dark, haunting the old diner.

When Lucy died, her killer had never been brought to justice for her murder. In Amanda's experience, this created the perfect paranormal recipe for spirits of the dead to be unable to cross over. Searching out Lucy's ghost seemed the only way to gain the information she and Phillip would need, and perhaps to bring a killer to justice and put an end to Lucy's wanderings.

The diner was now a severely neglected building, the wind and blowing sand having peeled most of the paint off the sign and the gray, weathered wood siding. There was a rusting 1940s pickup truck, the tires missing, sitting on blocks under all four wheels beside the crumbling restaurant.

She traced the image of the diner on the screen with her index finger and sighed. At times like this she wished the man who once had been her favorite uncle, something until this moment she had forced herself to forget, had stayed as she remembered him...before...

A sob escaped her lips and then she began to weep uncontrollably.

***

Phillip stood in the lobby facing the street, watching two tumbleweeds being pushed along by the constant desert wind. There were no signs of the old man or woman; he was alone. Dressed in tan walking shorts, a navy-blue golf shirt, and white Nikes, he had a pair of sunglasses raised high on his forehead.

"Hey, Amanda, ready to go?"

"Hi, Phillip," Amanda said, stepping off the last of the staircase onto the worn oriental carpet.

Having changed into her exploration garb, she spun around showing off her white walking shorts, mustard-yellow blouse, and white, open-toed sandals. "What do you think?"

Her unpleasant mood when she last saw Phillip had disappeared. A good cry so often cleared out the cobwebs in her head. She hated being used; it ruined her day. It wasn't his fault her uncle had molested her.

Phillip had treated her like a princess and he deserved better treatment.

Phillip turned toward her, smiling like the Cheshire cat. What was he up to now?

"You look good enough to take out on the town." He cocked one eyebrow. "Especially in this town."

He was joking, of course, but she didn't really care where they went provided they did it together. "Oh, Mr. Swann, you say the naughtiest things."

He chuckled. "OK, Ms. Dark, let's go to the old diner and look for some clues. What do you say?"

She swallowed a sudden lump of fear. "Sounds like a plan." She walked to stand beside him as he offered the crook of his arm. Grinning at him, she ran one hand around his offered elbow.

***

Amanda played the stream of white light from the heavy-duty flashlight gripped in her sweaty, pale hand over the inky interior of the deserted roadside diner. Her heartbeat was rapid and her dry mouth had a slightly metallic taste. Her tongue flicked over her lips.

She wondered where the ghost was hiding. It could be anywhere: in the walls, in the floor, in the kitchen cooking eggs. She swallowed a chuckle. This last was, of course, impossible. The power and water had been shut off after her uncle died.

It had taken an hour to walk to the diner at the edge of town near the highway. Her feet hurt and she was thirstier than she had ever been in her life, but Phillip seemed as fresh as when they'd set off.

He wanted to continue so she reluctantly agreed. Why couldn't they have brought the car?

When they'd arrived outside the diner, the sun had dropped to near the horizon. It would be dark in an hour. The doors and windows were boarded up, but together they managed to pry one of the boards off the front door to get inside. Not that it was all that difficult since the wooden boards and the wood door were dry and badly rotted by the desert conditions over the past two decades of neglect. Once inside, they had to use flashlights in order to see.

"We don't get a lot of customers these days," said a woman's voice coming from the their right.

A six-foot section of counter—a portion of which appeared to be have crumbled away due to rot—and six rusted, round, steel stools in front were all that remained of the original lunch counter. The fabric of the booths' seats beside the boarded-up windows was dusty and ripped, the stuffing hanging out in great clumps as if torn apart by wild animals.

The voice continued, "Not since they built the bypass."

"The bypass was built in 1962," whispered Phillip in Amanda's ear.

Amanda realized the voice must belong to Gib's first wife.

"Uh, Lucy? Is that you?" Swinging her flashlight beam, she discovered a woman standing behind the counter, a waitress dressed in a pink uniform skirt and matching blouse. Her fiery red curls were partially covered by a little, white-trimmed pink hat. In one hand she held a green-and-white order pad, in the other hand was a glass carafe filled with black coffee. Steam actually rose from inside the carafe.

The waitress—obviously a ghost as evidenced by her ivory, pale complexion and unblinking stare—wore a sardonic smile on her bloodless lips and her pale green eyes reflected curiosity.

"Yes. Are you two cops or sumthin'?" Lucy's ghost didn't wait for a response; instead, she grunted and took a step farther down the dusty counter away from them. She poured a measure of coffee into a dusty, white china mug on the counter.

Amanda assumed Lucy could see whoever was seated at the counter, but she couldn't. It was an odd restriction of her gift, something she had experienced a few times before: certain ghosts were echoes of the host after the spirit itself crossed over. It happened maybe one in a half million times, so while it wasn't that common, she had encountered it before.

Lucy's ghost recognized these echoes and thought they were as real as herself. Ghosts were unable to discern echoes from other ghosts. This particular echo must have been a customer of the diner.

"Why don't you cops move along and stop bothering old Barney and I. Ain't that right, Barney?" Lucy winked at the empty stool in front of the counter.

"Uh, Lucy—" began Amanda.

Lucy's ghost set the carafe on the counter and turned to glare at Amanda and Phillip, who both had their flashlights trained on her. "Do I know you people?" Amanda shook her head. "Then how do you know my name?"

Amanda hesitated. It was a good question and one that deserved a response. "Well, you see I'm Gib Dark's niece—"

Lucy's features were suddenly split by a wide grin and she rushed to stand in front of Amanda, the ghostly figure now sparkling under the light from the two flashlights.

"You're Mandy?" Lucy asked excitedly. "Well, why didn't you say so when you came in?" Lucy turned to look at the pass bar beyond which was the kitchen. "Hey, Gib, Mandy's here!"

Amanda froze. Her hands trembled, causing the flashlight beam to shake, and her heart beat rapidly. The swinging door separating the counter from the kitchen hung at an angle on one hinge. He'd have to pass through the wall...

A sudden wave of dizziness gripped her. Reaching out to grab the edge of the counter in order to steady herself made the beam of light wave about wildly. Phillip's flashlight also swung about crazily, so she knew he was experiencing the same thing as her.

The feeling quickly passed, but from the corner of one eye, Amanda saw the diner had started to physically change. Amanda's heart skipped a beat. The diner was transforming, somehow reverting to a past time when the diner had been new.

"Impossible," she whispered under her breath.

The weathered gray wall, the paint peeling from the crumbling plaster farthest away, straightened and became smooth and then changed from gray to a mint green. Next, the section of the counter that had been missing reappeared as if from nothing.

The white-gray speckled linoleum tiles on the floor looked freshly waxed. The light fixtures lining the ceiling changed from broken and rusted to gleaming stainless steel with glowing blubs. The light fixtures now looked to be newly installed.

As the wave touched the stools in front of the counter, they began to change from rusting relics to shiny new under the glow of the lights. Even the seat fabric of the booths against the windows and the stools, now a shiny aquamarine color, appeared to be brand-new with not one tear or mark.

Like a fast moving tsunami, the changes spread across the diner, racing toward them, unrelenting and undulating as if alive. As the wave of change was about to engulf them, Amanda closed her eyes and held her breath.

Nothing happened for several seconds, but she was too afraid to move.

"Hey, Mandy, what's wrong?"

Uncle Gib?

The soft burr of an air-conditioner motor sent a gentle breeze of cold air over her. When they first walked in, the musty, collapsing diner had been too warm and too humid. After releasing the air from her lungs, she sucked in a breath of the cool air. It felt so good.

Opening one eye, she saw a much younger version than she remembered of her Uncle Gib coming toward her through the now brand-new swinging door from the kitchen. With his square jaw and dark wavy hair, he looked as real and solid as if he were still alive. The man was grinning.

Sucking in another breath, she closed her eyes again as she struggled to steady her nerves. The transformation of an environment had never happened during a paranormal investigation. It was too incredible, too unbelievable to be real—but it was real.

How is this possible?

She opened both eyes to find herself looking into the coal black pupils of the man who had molested her. This man was her Uncle Gib.

***

Seated at the lunch counter, her bottom resting on the soft cushion, Amanda sipped from the clean glass of water held in her trembling fingers. Phillip sat on the stool beside her, sipping water from an identical glass, also filled with clear water. Her scream of shock still seemed to echo off the restaurant's walls.

Lucy and Gib stood leaning back against the waist-high fridges beneath the service counter built into the wall behind them. To their right, in the wall, was an opening with the stainless steel pass bar, where prepared food was placed awaiting pick-up by a waitress. Three heat lamps ran along the top edge of the opening, shining down on the pass bar to keep the orders warm until they were picked up.

As if Amanda's aunt and uncle weren't in the room, Phillip asked her to explain the transformation of the diner's interior, but she was unable to offer any explanation since she'd never seen this happen before. It surprised her he was able to see it happen, too. This was way beyond her experience or expertise and, she was afraid to admit, it frightened her.

The diner now looked brand-new as if they had been transported to 1957, no longer in 2014. Time travel was impossible, so she concluded this was some sort of paranormal event unlike anything she'd ever witnessed.

"Ummm," she began, her voice tentative, "Uncle Gib, did you build the diner?"

Uncle Gib focused his black eyes on her and nodded. "Yes, me and Lucy did all the work ourselves with our own four hands." His eyes were humorless and his tanned forehead was marred by a frown.

After the diner was regenerated (Amanda decided the word regenerated best described what they'd witnessed), Gib and Lucy had become fully human again, but in their younger bodies. They looked as real and alive as Amanda and Phillip; even their cheeks were flushed as if they had blood in their veins.

Amanda's well-tuned sense for all things paranormal told her that, when they left the diner, it would revert to its former dilapidated condition. She wished she had an explanation for all this that made some sense.

My gift really messes with my head some days.

Fortunately, she'd seen enough weird things on this job that one more strange, unexpected happening eventually seemed normal on some level.

"I'm so sorry, Uncle Gibb," she said, finally able to look her uncle in the eyes.

Gib shrugged but both he and Lucy didn't look happy. "You scared away all our customers," blurted Lucy. "We have bills to pay, ya know."

Gib shifted his gaze to his wife and placed one hand on her shoulder. "Take it easy, honey. Mandy's always been high-strung."

As if struck by a bolt from a blue sky, an idea suddenly struck Amanda. "If this is the fifties, then I haven't been born yet. How would you know what I'm like?"

Gib winced. Grinning sheepishly, he said, "I don't know, Mandy. I have access to all of the memories from my corporeal existence. Even..." his voice trailed off as his cheeks flushed crimson.

A familiar tingle of anger swelled in Amanda's belly but she forced it down. Anger would only lead to more pain. Now that she had him in front of her, she might finally get the answers she'd been seeking all her life. "Yes, of course...I'm curious about your death and Lucy's—" She stopped, uncertain if she should break the news of Lucy's murder to the victim.

Lucy slammed a fist into Gib's shoulder, causing him to wince in pain. "How does she know about that?"

Gibb shrugged.

I guess she knows already. "It's OK, Lucy," Amanda said, "I found an envelope containing a letter from Gib in my father's files after he died." She eyed her uncle, who appeared very much alive. Death seemed a debatable concept right now, so she decided not to tell Lucy about Gib's suicide. She sensed Lucy didn't know everything about her husband, which actually made sense since she died before Gib crawled into a whiskey bottle and before he molested Amanda.

"Anyway, regardless of our present circumstance, I know, Lucy, you were murdered, based on the contents of Uncle Gib's letter. He claims he was an undercover operative for the Arizona State Police and someone was sending him a message by killing you."

Gib nodded, his head dropping to his chest. "She's right." His voice was barely audible.

Lucy's pale features twisted in anger as she raised her fist and hit him in the shoulder again, this time much harder than before. "You son of a...you used me...Milt killed me, didn't he?"

Gib groaned and wrapped his injured arm with his left hand.

"Didn't he!" Lucy arms were at her sides, her hands curled into fists.

Gib nodded but remained silent.

"Uh, who's, Milt?' asked Amanda. She thought about asking about the gangsters mentioned in the trial transcript, but she wanted to hear this first.

Lucy looked at her. "Milt was his partner on the police force. I've never met anyone so jealous as that pig." She shuddered. "An awful man; crude, drank too much...he craved violence, ya know?"

"Was this before or after you started the diner?' asked Phillip.

Lucy stepped away from her cowed husband, crossing her arms over her chest.

"Not that it matters now, but Gib started this diner to escape his old job as a cop." She shifted her eyes to glare at Gib, who avoided her. "We were tired of the danger, the late nights, no days off, his crazy partner...all of it. Frankly, if Gib didn't leave the state police, we were through."

"Where can we find this Milt?" asked Phillip.

Gib looked at Amanda through bloodshot eyes. "Milton Spender lives in a nursing home in Phoenix." Her uncle looked so sad she couldn't help but feel sorry for him. Before she dealt with the problem with Lucy, she needed to air some family laundry.

"Uncle Gib..." she began, the old dark fear rising from within closed her throat. Pushing her fear aside she continued. "Uncle Gib, why did you molest me?"

He stuffed his hands in the pockets of his white cook pants while avoiding her eyes. "I'm so sorry, Mandy. I was drunk. I had a problem." He hesitated. "I told your father what happened, promising never to return to Boston." He locked eyes with her, his filled with tears. "I know it's not an acceptable excuse, but please, please forgive me. I've loved you like the daughter I never had since I first saw you at the hospital when you were born."

His eyes pleaded with her for forgiveness. Slowly the fear that had consumed her life, the shame that had ermeated her soul since she was twelve years old began to recede. After more than two decades, a terrible burden lifted from her shoulders.

She looked at Phillip, hoping he might help her to decide, but since he hadn't known how badly her uncle hurt her until this moment, he couldn't really help. He hadn't lived with this terrible secret. He gazed at her with sad eyes, a weak smile on his lips. While she sensed Phillip's sympathy, only she could decide.

"All right, Uncle Gib..." Her words caught in her throat and a shiver ran down her spine, but she pushed herself through the fear. "I'll...forgive you..."

A sudden feeling of pure joy shot from her toes to her head. Her words had set her free from the past. Her paranormal senses tingled, signaling she had done the correct thing by forgiving someone who so impacted her life.

Gib buried his head in his hands and began to sob while Lucy stroked his back. She looked at Amanda. "Thank you," she said softly.

Turning away, Phillip wrapped her in his arms, pulled her to him, and stroked her shoulder. She rested her head against his chest, feeling the steady beating of his heart.

"We have to visit this Milton Spender," she said. "Lucy needs our help."

Phillip chuckled lightly. "That's my girl, always thinking of others." He released her and grasped her shoulders with both hands, gazing into her eyes. "How're you doing?"

"I've never felt better in my life," she said and meant it.

***

Driving through the iron gates of the retirement community where Milton Spender lived, Amanda saw nothing like the retirement homes she'd seen before, or even imagined a retirement community could be. The sprawling, perfectly manicured facilities had to be exclusive to the very, very rich. No one of middle-class means could afford such a place, so how would a retired cop be living in such a community?

Designed around a massive park with sprawling flower beds of roses, gardenias, and mature rhododendrons, all covered with red, white, and yellow flowers, the community had tennis courts, an Olympic-sized pool, and even a full, eighteen-hole golf course. The magnificent grounds reminded Amanda more of a five star resort than a place where old folks went to die.

Amanda had forgotten to ask Uncle Gib about the gangsters, but decided it was too thin a line to follow since Lucy and Gib seemed adamant Milt Spender was the killer. Still, something niggled at the back of her mind telling her something wasn't right, but she couldn't put a finger on what was bothering her.

They parked under the breezeway covering the entrance and entered the lobby through the twin glass doors after a female valet took the keys for their rental car, saying she would park it for them.

The lobby smelled of lemon floor polish. Gleaming marble tiles covered the floor, finally ending at a massive reception desk. Behind the desk sat a man with slicked-back black hair cut close to his large head, wearing a white nurse's uniform. As they approached the desk, Amanda spotted a nametag over his left breast pocket that read C. Reddick.

Forcing her best glad-to-meet-you smile on her lips as they arrived at the desk, she said, "Hello. We're looking for Milton Spender."

Reddick, whose black eyes were focused on a document on the desk, looked up at them. "Milt? Why would you want ta see that old son of a bitch?"

Startled for a few seconds that Reddick would speak of a resident this way, Amanda waited several seconds before speaking. "Uh, well, we have an old friend who knows Milt and wants us to check in on him." Her mouth formed a weak smile. "To see if he's OK."

Reddick snorted derisively and rose from the chair he'd been sitting in. "It's your funeral, lady." He walked to stand in front of a bulletin board affixed to the wall behind him. After scanning a document pegged to the board, he said, "Milt should be in the music appreciation class—that is, if he felt like it today." He grunted. "Every day's an adventure with Milt."

Shaking his head, he walked back to sit in the chair. "Got ID?"

Phillip pulled out his wallet while Amanda opened her purse and extracted her driver's license from a pocket inside. After Reddick looked over their identification, he asked them to sign their names in a visitors' register.

"Folks from Boston come all the way to Phoenix to see a bastard like Milt Spender..." He snorted again. "Makes no difference to me, but you've come a long way for nuthin'." He handed them each a fire-engine-red plasticized visitor's pass with a clip to attach to their breast pockets, instructing them to display them at all times while on the premises.

"Thank you, Mr. Reddick. Which way to the class?"

Reddick pointed to the wide hallway left of the desk, filled with older men and women—some shuffling along aided by walkers, some in wheel chairs, others in track suits walking briskly along, their sport shoes squeaking on the tiled floor. To a person, they all appeared happy and content. "Follow the yellow line on the wall to G wing, Room 128A."

Amanda turned to face Phillip. Lowering her voice so Reddick couldn't hear them, she said, "Why don't you find a place for a coffee? I want to speak with Mr. Spender by myself." Phillip opened his mouth to speak until she placed one finger over his lips. "No questions, please. I need to do this alone."

Phillip nodded but his eyes told her he wasn't happy about her decision. Nevertheless, he disappeared in the opposite direction after asking a passing nurse for the location of the cafeteria.

Amanda watched him go, her stomach jumping to its own beat since her nerves were on edge. This case had given her a nervous stomach. She hadn't been sleeping well since starting the trek to Arizona, and meeting her uncle and aunt's younger ghosts hadn't helped her condition. True, a major emotional weight had been lifted from her after she forgave Gib, but she had the sinking feeling this visit to Milt wasn't going to end well.

She made her way along the maze of hallways following the yellow line painted on the wall until she found G wing. A sign with arrows under the big letter *G* showed room 128A was to the left.

Taking in a deep breath, she headed down the hallway, letting the air escape her lungs and taking another deep breath as she walked. She passed a number of the white-haired residents, all of whom nodded as they offered her close-mouthed smiles. With all the smiling, Amanda began to wonder if this was the Stepford seniors' home and all these people were duplicates created by computers and microchips.

The nurses she passed, on the other hand, didn't even look in her direction, causing her to wonder about the effectiveness of the security system. In Amanda's line of work, you tend to look at the details of a place when entering unknown territory. Often the minutiae of a place told you more than the people or the larger, more elaborate elements.

Staff who ignored the most basic security protocol showed they couldn't care less about the place where they worked and its residents, or the security personnel were incompetent, lazy, or both.

Sure enough, a portly man appeared from around a corner, coming in her direction, wearing black slacks and a white shirt with shoulder patches reading Security. His blond hair was cut to half an inch from his round head. He rode a Segway. Dark sunglasses hid his eyes and the belt around his waist was heavy with all sorts of rattling tools and numerous leather pouches.

He rolled to a stop beside her. The portable radio on his belt was on a low volume, but she could still hear snatches of conversations; something about a big game of some kind, and someone else talking about what they were making for dinner that night.

"Hey there, Miss, you got a visitor pass?"

Amanda showed him the visitor badge clipped to the hem of her shirt.

"OK, thank you, Miss." He nodded and headed away, soon disappearing in an adjacent hallway.

Watching the security guard until he disappeared, she finally shook her head. "Yup, that's a poor excuse for security. You called it, girl," she murmured.

Finally she found room 128A and, after opening the door, stuck her head inside. The room was large; no doubt it could seat at least fifty people at tables comfortably. There were no windows and the walls were lined with billboards from famous Broadway shows.

At the front of the room was a row of five occupied wheelchairs. In front of them was a raised platform, upon which stood a rail-thin, brown-haired man. Beside him was a small table where a mini stereo blared music.

Amanda recognized the tune being played. It was a song from the Broadway musical *Oklahoma*, the one about the fringe on top, or something like that. Her dad had loved those musicals and played the cast albums all the time when she was a young girl.

But right now she had more important things to take care of, like catching a murderer and helping two ghosts pass over.

One of the occupants of the wheelchairs had to be Milt Spender.

Stepping inside, she closed the door as softly as possible so as not to disturb the audience's enjoyment of the show tunes echoing off the walls. She walked as softly as possible toward the platform until she stood behind the wheelchairs, the occupants of which were exclusively male.

How am I going to nail down which one is Spender without interrupting the class?

It was then she noticed that the man on the platform was glaring at her, his brow marred by deep creases. He was trying to get her attention by mouthing something she didn't understand. She raised her hands in mock surrender and shrugged.

Walking around to stand in front of the wheelchairs, she studied each grizzled man. Two were thin, two were heavy, and one was medium. The three bears of the seniors set.

One had a scar on his left cheek, one had wispy gray hair that touched his shoulders, and one was bald as a cue ball. Her nose wrinkled at the overpowering odor of garlic emanating from Cue Ball.

The man at the end of the row glared at her with red-rimmed azure eyes. Unshaven, wearing a dirty, red-and-brown plaid nightgown over sky-blue pajamas, he propped bare feet on the footrests of the wheelchair. He seemed the most likely candidate to be a retired cop. His eyes followed her as she walked toward him. Yup, cop.

"Milt?" she whispered after stepping up to stand over him.

He grimaced. "What the fuck do you want?"

His tone suggested aggression, but his hands, buried in his lap, were trembling. And his head wobbled like a bobble head. Minutiae reveals truth.

"Let's you and me get out of here, Milt. We need to talk." She sensed all she needed to do was push him a little harder and he'd be putty in her hands.

Milt avoided her steady gaze. "I'm not going anywhere with you, bitch." He spat the words from between his cracked, dry lips, but his words lacked forcefulness.

She moved so she stood in front of him again, but he snapped his head in the other direction as if trying to escape. "Really?" she said. "Would you prefer we conducted our business in here?"

Milt's eyes shifted to lock with hers. There was fear behind them. "No...I mean...not really..." He reached down to unlock the brake on his chair and then began to wheel away using his hands to push the tires forward.

She glanced at the man on the platform and nodded. He raised the index finger of his left hand. What a nice guy.

Amanda followed Milt out the door into the corridor, then down the hall until they arrived at a door with a picture of him, his name written underneath in block letters. The picture of him looked pretty much identical to the man seated in the wheelchair.

Milt slapped a stainless steel plate on the wall next to the door and it began to slowly open into the room. As the gap became wider, the florescent lights in the ceiling inside flickered to life.

When the door had opened sufficiently, Milt turned his head slightly to catch her eye, grunted, then turned to face forward. He rolled himself inside.

Amanda followed him in, watching him until he stopped at the window overlooking the golf course where, in the distance, one gray-haired man was striking his golf ball while another man of a similar vintage watched from a powered cart.

It was sunny outside but Milt's room was located under an overhang, so very little sunlight came through the window.

Milt's elbows rested on the wheelchair's armrests, his hands clasped in front of him; clasping, unclasping, worrying themselves with nervous energy. He peered at the golfers, his body trembling uncontrollably. "I always knew this day would come," he said, his voice soft as sun-warmed butter. "Are you going to kill me now?"

Amanda snorted, causing him to look at her, surprise registering on his gaunt, unshaven features. "Milt, I'm not here to kill you. I'm here to help Lucy and Gib Dark."

Milt shifted his bottom in his wheelchair. "Gib? Lucy? They're—"

"Dead," she finished for him. "Yes, they are, but their ghosts are very much still around, and they don't want to be around, for lack of a better term that would make some sense to a layperson such as yourself."

Milt had stopped shaking, the fear beginning to dissipate. "Sorry, I don't follow..."

She nodded and moved to sit on the single bed facing him. "Gib claims you killed his wife, Lucy. I need to know if you did." She leaned toward him, her eyes on his. "It's just that easy." Now that she was closer, she detected the sour smell of sweat coming from Milt. She wondered when he had last bathed.

Milt was gaining confidence now, his arrogance returning. "I used to be a cop, ya know."

She smirked. "Yes, I know. You were Gib's partner." She looked
out the window. "From the look of this place, I'd say you were a
corrupt cop."

Milt's eyes narrowed. "How would you know?"

Amanda chuckled. "Let's stop playing games, Milt. Just answer
my question: did you murder Lucy Dark?"

"Lady, I have no idea who the fuck you are, so I'm not gonna tell
you shit."

"From what I see, Milt, my boy, you may need my services
sooner than later."

"Oh, yeah, really? So who and what are you that a useless old
man like me would require your services?"

Amanda grinned. "I'm Amanda Dark. I'm Gib's niece and I'm
a paranormal investigator. I also have a special talent helping spirits
of the dead unable to cross over after their death due to unresolved
issues while they were alive." The grin faded from her lips and she
turned her attention to Milt. "You're dying. From your appearance,
I'd say most likely cancer."

Milt's eyes went wide and watery. "How did you know?"

"I know all, I see all, sorta like a modern-day Wizard of Oz,
only I don't hide behind a curtain." She paused to consider her next
words, then she had an idea.

"Listen, Milt, I'll make you a deal. If you tell me who killed
Lucy, I'll help you cross over when the time comes."

One corner of Milt's mouth curled slightly. "Who said I'd have
any problem crossing over?"

"Trust me, Milt, I'm a professional. I always know." Amanda
paused to wait for Milt to mull over her offer. Truth was, she had no

idea if he'd have problems; she didn't know enough about him.

She made her offer on the scant bits of details she'd gleaned after meeting him, her special intuition, and what Gib and Lucy had said about him.

It wasn't much to go on, but she was betting even if she missed the mark she'd at least have nicked a corner of truth.

Milt might not actually want to go wherever it was he was headed after death if he was a crooked cop and a murderer. In her experience, the afterlife was never what people expected, or so her spirit contacts told her.

Milt moved his wheelchair slightly back from the window, the tires making a soft *brr* sound on the tiles. His head hung down to his chest. "OK, but please help me. I've done some stuff I'm not proud of..." His voice dropped off and a gasp escaped his lips. He looked up into her eyes, trails made by tears running down his sunken cheeks.

Her heart ached for him. This man suffered from terrible, soul-crushing pain. She resolved to help him no matter what it took.

"Why don't you tell me everything," she said softly.

In a halting voice, Milt began his story.

Amanda listened, intent on words filled with raw emotion concerning things he obviously hadn't talked about in a very long time.

She was right about his terminal cancer. Since Milt was nearing his eighty-ninth birthday, he had already accepted the inevitable end.

He assured Amanda he hadn't killed Lucy. Though he was jealous of Gib and thought Lucy was too good for his partner, he couldn't hurt either of them. Years after Gib left the police force, Milt and his new partner had been offered substantial bribes from drug dealers to look the other way.

Since his finances had been wiped out in a real estate scam and his wife had left him, he had decided he deserved to retire in style, so he accepted the offers and managed to accrue a significant amount of money. "I was wrong. Money isn't what's important in life," he said.

He then explained that while he didn't kill Lucy, he knew who did, but had been threatened with exposure of his corruption if he revealed the truth. He'd remained silent since that time.

Amanda's heart rate increased. Now she was getting somewhere. "Who wanted to send Gib a message by murdering his wife?"

Milt looked down at the floor. "That's what he always believed, but it wasn't true. The killer wasn't sending him any message..." His voice caught.

"OK, so if that wasn't the motive, then why?"

Milt sighed, his breath shaky. "Someone wanted Lucy for himself... someone powerful...dangerous. When Gib and Lucy said no, he threatened to kill her."

"Who?"

He looked up at her through bloodshot eyes. He opened his mouth to answer but the intercom speaker in the ceiling cut him off. The announcer's voice was feminine, nasally, and slightly annoying. "Residents, there are now lemon cookies and green tea available in the cafeteria where we will be starting the bingo game shortly. So join your fellow residents for a fun-filled afternoon."

As the announcer spoke, Amanda stood and walked to the window overlooking the golf course, her shoes scuffing over the tile. Watching two new golfers swinging at their balls reminded her what a silly game golf really was.

When the announcer finished, she shifted her eyes to look at Milt and froze. His face was the color of a concord grape. He gasped for breath, his gnarled hands clasping at his throat.

Her heart beating rapidly, Amanda searched frantically for the call button to summon assistance. Finally her eyes landed on a panel with three colored buttons on the wall over the single bed crammed into an alcove. She hurried to the panel and pressed the black button marked NURSES' STATION. Nothing happened.

There was a speaker on the panel under the buttons. The label under blue button to the left of the black button said it was for the intercom. Pressing the button and holding it in, Amanda shouted into the speaker. "Help! I need help!"

After she released the button, a man's sluggish voice replied. "All right, lady, take it easy."

"No, you don't understand..."

Milt had begun to make choking noises and he shuddered as air rushed from his lungs. Then his eyes rolled back in his head.

Amanda froze, her eyes wide with horror as Milt's gnarled hands frantically undid the seat belt holding him in the chair. He tried to stand, but instead he slumped forward until finally collapsing to the floor. First on his knees until he dropped on his belly, his face bouncing off the tiles with his arms and legs sprawled out from his torso and bent at unnatural angles.

Milton Spender was dead.

***

Amanda joined Phillip in the cafeteria, where he sat alone at one end of a table large enough for ten people, with a cinnamon bun and a white ceramic mug in front of him. Amanda was relieved there were very few people in the cafeteria at this time of day since it was just after two o'clock in the afternoon.

The last thing she needed was anyone to overhear their conversation and then have to explain it. Most people did not understand or appreciate her work.

She could see a few bites were missing from the cinnamon bun but the remainder was untouched. The mug, which she saw contained black coffee, was half empty—or was it half full?

"No good?" she asked, nodding at the bun after sitting in an empty chair across from Phillip.

"Terrible," he said. "Dry as the dust in a vacuum cleaner bag and the icing is so sweet it hurts your teeth." He shrugged and raised the mug to his lips to take a sip. "Coffee's OK, though."

"Milt's dead."

Phillip had raised his mug intending to take another drink of coffee, but stopped a few inches from his mouth, the mug floating. "What? How?"

"He was terminal." She shrugged. "It was just a matter of time."

Looking away so he couldn't see the sadness in her eyes, she cleared her throat. The truth was, she had never gotten used to death no matter how much she experienced in her job. And Milt's end was truly terrible.

She secretly hoped she never would get used to it since helping the dead had been her motivation to become a paranormal investigator in the first place.

"Wow," said Phillip before he took a generous drink of coffee, then set the mug on the table. "Did he say anything important before he died?"

She nodded, still avoiding him. "He said someone else wanted Lucy for themselves, and when she wouldn't agree, he threatened to kill her."

"So who was this person?"

Amanda turned to face him and sighed. "He was about to tell me when..."

Phillip snorted and his mouth formed a crooked smile. "Yeah, he was cut off just like in the movies. I'm surprised there wasn't a knife sticking from his back."

"A man is dead, Phillip, this is no time for jokes."

Phillip winced. "Yeah, I'm sorry, Amanda, but death makes me a little goofy. I'll stop. But really, any idea who he might have been talking about?"

She nodded, her eyes drifting to the vacant chair next to him, then moving back to him. "Actually, there were several gangsters in the trial transcript Gib said may have been the murderer."

Phillip arched a single eyebrow. "Really? Any idea which one Milt might have known?"

"Oh, I expect he knew them all, but his ghost told me the name of one who was jealous of Gib and who threatened Lucy."

"Well, why didn't you say so before?"

"Because, my dear Phillip, Milt's ghost just sat down beside you and shared the name with me."

Phillip chuckled. Since partnering with Amanda on several cases, nothing shocked him anymore and he fully accepted her talents were very real. "I love it when you use your gift. It really is so cool."

Amanda ginned. "Thanks, partner. We're going to find Al "Stinky" Garbone, the man who allegedly murdered Lucy Dark."

She knew then she didn't need to find Stinky Al because the murder of Lucy was pure cause and effect. Amanda's paranormal senses told her something was rotten in Arizona. Neither Milt nor this faceless small-time wise guy, Stinky Al, killed Lucy. She knew now who committed the murder and who should pay the price.

**

Amanda entered the Moonrise Diner with Phillip a step behind her. Upon seeing the diner's interior, she pulled up short and he ran into her from behind, nearly causing her to stumble and fall. "Hey! Watch it."

"Sorry," Phillip said after stepping away from her. "What's up?"

"Look at this place," Amanda said, waving her arms at the pile of wood wreckage around them. It actually seemed worse than before.

Phillip scanned the restaurant. "Yeah, it looks like an old, dumpy, broken-down diner."

Amanda had never expected to find the diner shiny and new like when they left here last time, but the dilapidated condition of the long-abandoned building caught her off guard. Dust and mold covered every shattered booth, the rotting counters were weathered, and sand had blown in through the gaping holes in the walls.

She hadn't realized how bad it was inside before since it had been dark the last time they were here. In the daytime she worried the ceiling would fall on them any second. This wasn't so much a haunted diner as a had-it diner.

"Uh, Uncle Gib? Aunt Lucy?" Amanda stepped forward tentatively, unsure if the floor might collapse beneath her at any second. She froze when the floorboard under her creaked, followed by a loud, snapping sound.

Suddenly the broken down restaurant began to transform once again, beginning at the far wall.

Amanda closed her eyes as the wave of change came rushing toward her. Her heart pounded hard. Within seconds there was a soft

206

whirr and a cool breeze washed over her.

Opening one eye, she saw a smiling Gib standing behind the transformed lunch counter beside Lucy, who also grinned at her.

"Whew," she said, "I'm so glad to see you two." Amanda collapsed with relief on an empty stool while Phillip sat on the one next to her. She shot him a glance and saw his eyes looked as relieved as she felt. The diner had been regenerated before it fell on them.

"Do you have good news?" asked Gib, his handsome face eager as a child on his birthday.

"Sort of," began Amanda, uncertain how Gib and Lucy would accept the death of his old partner. Much like taking off a Band-Aid, it was best to pull it off in one go. "Milt's dead."

Gib's face sagged. "Really?"

Amanda nodded. "But I did manage to speak to him while he was still alive."

"So you killed him?" asked Lucy as she wiped the counter with a white cloth.

"No, of course not, I don't kill people. I just talk to dead people." She hesitated, realizing how ridiculous this sounded. But Gib and Lucy were ghosts and she was talking to them.

Gib glanced at Lucy. "Why don't you get them some coffee?"

Lucy nodded and walked to the stainless steel coffee brewer station standing on the service counter in front of the wall separating the kitchen from the counter area. The brewer had three warmers, each with a glass carafe containing black coffee. The two on the side warmers were half full; the one under the dispensing spout was three-quarters full.

Ghosts must drink a lot of coffee.

Lucy filled two white ceramic mugs, then came back to set them on the lunch counter in front of them.

"I'll get the creamer and the sugar," she said. She quickly returned with a stainless steel creamer with a hinged lid, a mint green ceramic bowl filled with white sugar, and two spoons.

Phillip looked at Amanda, his eyes curious. She shrugged, reached to grasp the mug, and realized it was warm. Raising the mug, she sipped the coffee and it tasted slightly nutty and rich. How was this possible?

Lucy looked anxious. "Is it OK?"

Amanda nodded. "Yeah, it's good."

Phillip raised his mug and took a small sip. His eyes went wide.

Amanda grinned and set the mug back on the counter. "As I was saying, I spoke to Milt and he told me who really murdered Lucy." Seeing the fear in Gib's ghostly eyes, she paused. It seemed every case brought new experiences. A ghost afraid? Who knew?

She cleared her throat, then continued. "Anyway, Milt says some guy named Stinky Al murdered Lucy—"

"I knew it!" Gib cut her off and turned to face his wife. "You and Al? Really?"

Lucy took two steps back from Gib, her body trembling, fear in her eyes. "Gib, it wasn't like that..."

Gib walked up to her and pressed an index finger into her chest "Really? You and Al were cheating on me behind my back, weren't you? You lousy whore! Slut!" It was then Amanda realized Gib had a chef"s knife gripped in his right hand. He stepped up and slashed the blade across Lucy's throat.

Since she was a ghost, her head separated from her body and floated in midair, but no blood came from the wound. "Gib!" Lucy's disembodied head screamed at her husband. "You bastard! You killed me again."

Amanda leaned closer to Phillip in order not to be heard. "I think it's time we exited stage left."

Phillip raised one eyebrow. "Huh?"

"Let's go and leave these two lovebirds alone."

They rose simultaneously from the stools and hurried to the door just as the diner began to change to its former state of about-to-collapse.

Once outside, they watched as the diner's four walls collapsed inward with a loud crash. Then the roof fell onto the pile of broken, weather-grayed wood, enveloping them in a cloud of dust and sand. The diner was now a pile of kindling.

"What just happened?" asked Phillip, coughing as the dust cloud settled over them. Trying in vain to brush off his tan shorts and cactus-green shirt, he turned to face Amanda, who shook her head to shake some of the dust out of her hair.

She snorted to clear her nostrils and spat sand from her mouth. "The end of the Moonrise Diner obviously, but also the truth."

"What truth?"

"Gib killed Lucy and got away with it. Blaming Milt, then Stinky Al—they were decoys, or maybe an excuse to fool himself, or to bury his guilt, or who knows why. Whatever the reasons, my Uncle Gib is exactly who he appeared to be."

"What now?"

Amanda smirked. "Well, I expect with the destruction of the diner, they've both crossed over." She scanned the wreckage. "Somehow I don't think Gib is much liking where he ended up."

Phillip stepped up and wrapped his arms around her. She hugged him back, feeling his heart beating against her chest. "What about you?" he asked softly.

"I'm better. Much better."

Whoever said the truth will set you free knew exactly what they were talking about, because Amanda Dark had never felt as free as she did right now.

About the Authors

Russ Crossley

An international selling author, Russ Crossley writes science fiction, fantasy, and mystery/suspense as well as their various subgenres. He has written several short stories and novels under the name R.G. Hart.

His latest science fiction satire set in the far future, *Revenge of the Lushites*, was released in the fall of 2013 and is a sequel to *Attack of the Lushites,* which was released in 2011. Both titles are available in e-book and trade paperback.

He has sold several short stories that have appeared in anthologies from various publishers, including WMG Publishing, Pocket Books, and St. Martin's Press.

He is a member of SF Canada and is past president of the Greater Vancouver Chapter of Romance Writers of America. He is also an alumnus of the Oregon Coast Professional Fiction Writers Master Class taught by award-winning author/editors Kristine Katherine Rusch and Dean Wesley Smith.

Feel free to contact him on Facebook, Twitter, or his website http:www.russcrossley.com. He loves to hear from readers.

Rita Schulz

Rita lives on the Sunshine Coast in British Columbia with Russ, her husband, who is also a fiction writer.

She has written for years and is an alumna of the Oregon Writers Network and the Greater Vancouver Chapter of the Romance Writers of America.

Her most recently published stories are *Fire in Their Hearts* with R.G. Hart from Champagne books, and *Ladies of the Jolly Roger* and *Tales of the Fantastic* from 53rd Street Publishing.

Please visit her website at http://www.ritacrossley.com to view her other works.

Selected titles from 53rd Street Publishing you may enjoy

For a more complete bibliography go to http://
www.53rdstreetpublising.com

Other titles by Russ Crossley

Razor and Edge Mysteries
The Kidnapping of Billy Buttons
String of Pearls
Death by Clown
Beggin' For Murder
Ragged Ice
The Grand Central Mystery
A Strange Case of Undead Murder

Jazz Stiletto Mysteries
A Day Without Sunshine
Skullduggery
Instrument of Justice (first published in *Over My Dead Body*
online mystery magazine)

The Amanda Dark paranormal mysteries
Hook Island
Grind Manor
Moonrise Diner
A Father's Daughter
My Partner the Zombie
Hungry For Your Love Anthology (St. Martin's Press)

The Trudy Wilson Mystery Novel Series
Bad Loyalty
Shear Murder
Buzzcut coming in 2015

Other Novels
Attack of the Lushites
Revenge of the Lushites
My Zombie Prince
Antique Virgin
The Fire In Their Hearts with R.S. Meger (from Champagne
Books)
Zomopolis
The Last Serial Killer

Other titles by Rita Schulz

Short Fiction
Blarney
Flower & Bird
Party Central
Once Upon a Time
The Scarlet Curse
Spoken Words
The Brownie's Holiday
A Little Old Fashioned
In The Land of Dragons
A Little Kitchen Magic
Silver Light

For Pete's Sake
Cleaning Up is Hard to Do
Confessions of a Bold Maiden
All for One
Lucky List
A Spark of Courage
Party Line
Spoken Words

Collections
Ladies of the Jolly Roger with Russ Crossley
Ten Tempting Tales with R.S. Meger
The Fantastic Five with R.S. Meger
Unique Tales of the Fantastic
Tales of the Fantastic

Novels
Fire In Their Hearts (with R.G. Hart from Champagne Books)

Another title from 53rd Street Publishing you may enjoy.

In the not-too-distant future, medical advances rid the world of serial killers forever—all except one, The Last Serial Killer.

That killer is about to wreak havoc. Using right-wing radio host and Gulf War III veteran Todd Road as an unwilling conduit to aliens who claim he's innocent, the killer gets out of prison.

Todd and FBI agent Angela Cody join forces to recapture the killer—encountering a bloody trail of bodies, a future America thrown into chaos by fear and confusion, and deadly marauders bent on murder—and following clues to a final, twisted, horrifying end.

A story of suspense blending murder and justice with a dash of science fiction unlike anything you've ever read.

"A futuristic, suspenseful page turner about a killer who enjoys his grisly work." — Rita Schulz, author of The Scarlet Curse.

The Last Serial Killer is available online in e-book and print formats from your favorite book retailer.

www.ingramcontent.com/pod-product-compliance
Lightning Source LLC
Chambersburg PA
CBHW031726170626
46808CB00005B/1904